A Serial
RAPIST

CLARENCE WILLIS

authorHOUSE®

AuthorHouse™
1663 Liberty Drive
Bloomington, IN 47403
www.authorhouse.com
Phone: 1-800-839-8640

First published by AuthorHouse   01/24/2012

ISBN: 978-1-4685-2330-0 (sc)
ISBN: 978-1-4685-2331-7 (ebk)

Printed in the United States of America

Any people depicted in stock imagery provided by Thinkstock are models, and such images are being used for illustrative purposes only.
Certain stock imagery © Thinkstock.

This book is printed on acid-free paper.

This book dedicated to my wife Hilda, my daughter Nancy, and our fellow residents here at Pinecrest Place whose kind words of encouragement keep me writing.

CONTENTS

Clarence Willis
1150 8th Avenue SW
Apartment 602
Largo, FL 33770
727 588 9036
kj4ej79@yahoo.com

Chapter One

THE SEAFORD CHIEF OF POLICE John Daley, called a press conference. He told the newspaper reporters that the infamous 'Class Reunion Murders' had been solved and all the suspects in those Seaford, Delaware1984 class reunion murders that were being held in jail had been released.

He reported that the murderer of the two women was proven to have been Horace Hastings and that Horace himself had been killed by Robert Adams of Salisbury, Maryland and that he was now in jail charged with the first degree murder of Horace Hastings.

After the complete story had been released to the reporters, Bill Carle the FBI agent who was in charge of the serial murder investigation of the three murders, placed a call to Helen Hastings, the widow of Horace.

He asked her to have dinner with him that evening because he had been ordered back to the Wilmington office of the FBI early the next day.

Bill and Helen had been very close friends and were very fond of each other over the two years they were both attending the University of Delaware. They had talked of getting married after they graduated, but they were not formally engaged. Bill was transferred for financial reason from the University of Delaware to the University of Tennessee after his family moved from Delaware to Tennessee.

They continued to correspond with each other for several months but Helen eventually started dating Horace Hastings, a Seaford high school classmate.

Helen's now deceased husband Horace, was a close friend of both Bill and Helen during Bill's two years at Delaware. Bill had dated Helen over the course of those two years and that led to his friendship with Horace.

About five months after Bill transferred to Tennessee, Helen started dating Horace and they were married in their senior year at the University. Bill never married.

In rather quick succession following and during Helen's first high school class reunion in June of 1989, three members of the class had been murdered, one of which was her husband Horace.

After the FBI was asked for assistance, by Chief Daley, in fear that a serial murderer was in the area, the FBI approved the request.

Bill now a special agent with the FBI, read the Seaford police report of the case, and after finding the names of his two old college friends Helen and Horace listed in the report, he requested his assignment to the case. It was approved and he arrived in Seaford the next morning.

His attraction to Helen resurfaced over the course of the lengthy investigation of the three murders and their love for each other was slowly renewed.

The first murder victim, Harriet Obrien's classmate Bob Miller and his wife Kathy Black had planned to marry after their graduation from high school in 1984; but unknown to Bob, Kathy was raped and impregnated by another youth in her senior year.

Kathy quit school and moved from Seaford to Jarrett, Virginia to live with her grandparents without telling Bob the truth as to why she was moving.

A few days after the rape, when Bob called her to go to a movie, she simply told him that she had found another boyfriend and didn't love him anymore. It was widely reported locally that she had eloped and moved south. Bob was devastated and after graduation left Seaford.

Three years later, after her grandmother died, she and her little son Norman returned to Seaford.

On her return to Seaford she told her friends that she was now divorced from her husband. No one questioned her statement. She found a job as the information clerk at the local library. She did not attend the class reunion because she had not graduated with the class.

It was after Bob's returned to Seaford to attend the class reunion that he and Kathy eventually got together again and they were soon married. They were now living in Stanton, Delaware where Bob was a partner in a computer web development company.

Bill Carle and Helen had been asked to stand up with Bob and Kathy at their wedding in Seaford and they agreed to do so after they were told that Bill was responsible for getting them back together again after six years.

Bill was, at that time, in charge of the investigation in the class reunion murders.

Bob was, at one time during the investigation, a suspect in those murders because he had been seen in Seaford the day before the reunion and had disappeared after the murders. He did not attend the reunion although he had paid his registration fee to attend.

It was later proven that Bob was actually in Virginia looking for Kathy, because he had been told that she was divorced and no longer married. He had been told that she was living in Jarrett, Virginia after she left Seaford but he was not told that she was now back in Seaford.

Kathy had been living with her grandparents and had actually not married anyone. She didn't want anyone, especially Bob, to know that she had been raped and was pregnant when she left Seaford.

A few months after she and Bob finally got together they married as they had originally planned six years earlier.

Helen's daughter and Kathy's son were participants in Bob and Kathy's wedding.

When the so called Class Reunion Murders cases were officially closed after almost a year of investigation, Bill told Helen over dinner, that he was to appear before a news conference the next morning in Wilmington, Delaware for the purpose of accepting his promotion to the position of Special Agent in Charge of the FBI Branch office in Wilmington, Delaware.

The position of Bureau Chief was one that Bob was hoping for. He was hoping for a position that would allow him more personal and family time.

Helen told him how proud she was that he was to be promoted and added, "Does that mean that you will be leaving Seaford soon and have that bureau chief's job you were looking for?"

"Yes it does, my work here in Seaford has been completed. I do love you and I am hoping that you and your two children will come to Wilmington with me."

"I will now spend most of my time in an office rather than being in the field on an assignment. I will be free to have some family time that I don't have now. I do hope you will join me in Wilmington. If you wish we can even live in New Castle near your new job at the high school."

Helen had just been told that she had been hired by the New Castle County school board to fill a position working with children with learning disabilities in New Castle, Delaware."

"Is that some kind of proposal Bill? Are you asking me to marry you?"

"Yes, I am Helen, I love you. Will you marry me?"

"I do love you Bill but I just would have expected you would have asked me on a bended knee. I will marry you; but are you certain that you can handle becoming the father of my two children? Both of them love you as much as I do? That sure will be a big change in your life style. Are you sure you can handle that?"

"Yes as I have told you before, I love them both. I can't wait to become a father to them. I am hoping that after we are married, you will agree to have a judge legally change their last names to Carle and to legally let me adopt them, They are both young enough for us to eliminate the constant queries of their having a different last name then ours."

"Bill, that's a wonderful idea. That will be a great help to them in reducing those queries. If it is okay with you, I would like for Bob Miller and Kathy to stand up with us? After all we did stand up with them."

"Whoa there Helen, I haven't given you your ring yet. On a bended knee you ask?"

He lowered himself to his right knee and again asked, "My dear Helen, the love of my life, the mother of two beautiful children that I want as my own, Wilt thou have this old beau to be your wedded husband?"

Laughing, Helen said, "I will." Bill handed her the box holding the ring.

"Bill, I didn't think that a stiff old FBI agent like you could be that funny?"

"Stiff huh? You haven't seen how stiff I can be yet; but you will find that out as soon as we are married."

"Oh wow! What do you think about what I said about Bob and Kathy and the children?"

"That's a great idea Helen, and our children and Kathy's son can repeat their roles for us in our wedding just as they did in Bob and Kathy's wedding."

"I'm so excited, I know that Nancy will be as excited as I am and as she was, when asked to be in Bob and Kathy's wedding. We can surely find a part for Doug to perform something in our wedding. Remember how he felt when he was the only child not in Kathy's wedding? Perhaps he can help spread the flowers or even give me away to you. Yes, that's it I'll let him give me away"

Three weeks later Bill and Helen were married at the Pike Creek Valley Country Club and after the reception, they dropped off the children Nancy and Doug to stay with the Millers. The three children were very happy to see each other again.

Bill and Helen then left on a flight to Aruba for a two week honeymoon.

After arriving in Aruba and checking in at their hotel and after a great seafood dinner, they spent the evening in their room overlooking the ocean.

"Bill it's been a long time since I was last with Horace."

"Not as long as I have waited for you I've been waiting since college days remember."

"Bill, do you agree with the prosecuting attorney's report that Jeanne and Harriet were truly murdered by Horace?"

"Yes I do Helen, all the evidence certainly points to Horace having done it. If you will remember a piece of wire and blood stains on his gloves were found in Horace's old pickup truck. That with Steve Cockran's testimony about the red convertible found in Laurel after Harriet's death was pretty conclusive. The DNA also indicated that Horace had sex with both women before they were killed. Why do you ask? I thought that you too had suspected Horace at the time."

"Yes Bill, I did suspect Horace at the time; but I still just cannot convince myself that Horace could have done such a thing. I do know for certain that he was doing all those other things he was reported having done, like his sleeping with them; but I just can't conceive him murdering anyone. Why did he rape them if they were having sex with him?"

"I still feel that there is some reasonable doubt on the murders. Horace rarely used that truck, and maybe the wire and gloves were placed in the truck by someone else to give the appearance that Horace did it. I never knew Horace to wear gloves."

"Horace was a good father and his love for our two children was actually the root cause of our troubles in the divorce proceedings. I am certain, that with time, we could have worked out a divorce arrangement. A lot of the prosecuting people thought money was his motive for their murders. In my opinion that was not the motive."

"Horace and his lawyers never offered or mentioned to me any kind of money arrangement, other than their suggestion that most of any monetary award should be placed in trust for the children. Horace had asked for that and I had agreed."

"Our real differences were over our other assets, the poultry business, the rental properties, and the farm properties. After all, it was my parent's loan and gift that got us started in the business. I was more concerned with the problem of his wanting custody of the children then I was on the money matters. I didn't want them exposed to his 'way of life' all his whoring around and drinking. That is all we were really fighting about."

"After all, I did give most all of our assets back to his family didn't I? I just can't get the thought of his being a murderer out of my mind."

"I truly feel he just couldn't have murdered those women. I think that there was more to the case then that. If it was for money, I think that at least he would have made some kind of offer in that area. He never did."

"Yes, I understand your feeling Helen; but I guess we will never know for certain whether he did or did not because the state prosecutor accepted the information that had been collected; and of course there was no jury trial that would have demanded proof beyond a reasonable doubt, because Horace of course was not alive to defend himself. We were at a dead end with the case. All the evidence did point to Horace."

"Yes, I understand that Bill, but one is considered innocent until proven guilty without a reasonable doubt aren't they? I do wish there had been more evidence to prove to me that he actually did it."

"Even though I can't understand why Horace was in Laurel at the time Steve said he went to Laurel to pick him up. In my opinion, that still doesn't prove without a doubt that he killed the girls."

"If I had that answer perhaps I would feel differently and it would help me get over Horace's guilt. I just can't stop thinking that there is more to those deaths and Horace's involvement."

"I know you are sweetheart, but there was absolutely nothing presented or found that let us think otherwise. We were satisfied that he had done it. I don't think there is any really serious animosity toward Horace locally. The state's attorney simply felt that there was no reason to go any further with the investigation or to trial."

"Yes, I am aware of that; but I just hate for Nancy and Doug to grow up thinking that their father was a murderer when there is so much of the testimony that was really not proven. Anyone could have placed those items in Horace's pickup truck. He rarely ever used that truck. I have a feeling that the glove and that bloody wire were placed there to make it look like Horace did it and the killer knew that Horace's marital problems would help in doing that."

"Yes, there is that possibility but again, that wire was taken off a roll of identical wire used in his broiler houses on the feed conveyors."

"Helen regarding the children, it will be our job to bring them up as a happy family and I think in time those memories will soon disappear. But let's begin by trying to put the matter out of our minds completely. The past is history. Remember we are on our honeymoon. Shall I order a bottle of wine be sent up here to our room?"

"That's a good idea. Let's get into something more comfortable."

"I hope it's a sexy red nightgown."

"Oh dear, don't tell me you don't like black?"

Chapter Two

FRED MESSICK READ ABOUT HIS rape and murder of the two Seaford girls in the morning newspaper. He was in a very depressed mood. He had been sick all night. He had lost the only girl that he ever loved and had killed two women. He read in the paper about Horace and Helen's marital troubles and remembering that he had helped paint Horace's broiler house roof.

He got an idea that perhaps he could make it appear that Horace had committed his own crimes, if he placed the wire and gloves he used in that old truck of Horace's that he had used to go get some more paint.

He was terribly upset with himself. He had no right to treat those two girls like that. They had nothing to do with his Jennifer refusing to go to Florida with him where he could find work.

Years ago in his early teens, he had raped two girls when he was a student in West Virginia but he had never killed anyone. He had started several other attempts to rape a girl but had always fought off the urge until he met Harriet. She was a stranger. She did not know who he was and he didn't have to fear her telling on him. He wanted her and he was going to leave the area anyway.

He was sure he could not be connected to her. She surely didn't know him and he had never been seen with her.

He did know the two girls in West Virginia but they were different, both were known to have had sex with many of his friends. He was determined to get on their lists.

He could always claim that they had consented even if they had not. He would have made that claim if they had reported being raped. He was right—they did not tell and they didn't put up much of a fight.

He was irritated when they first refused him and he forced himself on them. After completion of the rape of the first of those two girls, the girl did nothing to let him believe that she would tell anyone about him raping her. He even took the first girl to a local restaurant after the rape and they had a sandwich and a drink together. They parted in friendly terms and she told him, "Maybe we can get together again sometime." Still, he had raped her.

They did get together several times after that night but now there was only consensual sex. He was not as excited as when he had raped her.

The second girl that he raped in West Virginia was a friend of the first girl. He approached her a month or so later and asked her to go to a drive in movie with him. She agreed. After the movie he drove to a wooded area where he attempted to have sex with her and when she refused he forcefully raped her.

Like her friend, she did not report the rape. He had told her that he would deny it if she did, and he would tell the police about all the other boys that she had sex with. He didn't know any such boys, but he had been told that she had done so.

He approached both of the girls later at various times and had consensual sex with both of them. He learned from them that he enjoyed raping the girls more than he did when they openly had sex with him. He was aroused by the thought of a struggle.

He quit seeing both of those two girls and soon moved to Delaware with his family and graduated from the Laurel High School in Laurel, Delaware. He never raped a girl again until he saw Harriet in a deli parking lot in Seaford, Delaware getting in her new red convertible sports car.

After his fiancé Jennifer had refused to go to Florida with him because he did not have a job, he started drinking and decided that he didn't need a wife anyway. He knew he could always rape a girl anytime he wanted and of course there were prostitutes.

He could select any girl he wanted. It was easy, and he remembered the joy he got when he had raped those two West Virginia girls. He was in complete control—A great feeling that he thoroughly enjoyed.

He was going to drown his miseries before he left for Florida after Jennifer had refused to go with him. He spent the afternoon drinking in a bar in downtown Seaford with a friend, who left him at the bar when it came time to leave.

Fred had wanted to stay and drink and was enjoying throwing darts at the dartboard with the other men. He had won over ten dollars.

Fred had no car to get home in and when told by his friend they had to go home. "You go ahead—not a problem I'll get a ride home."

Later that evening Harriet drove to a local deli after leaving a baby shower party given for a friend and classmate.

As Fred walked into the parking lot of the deli to call his roommate on the public phone to come get him; he struck up a conversation with Harriet about her new red convertible sports car.

He did not know Harriet but they got into a conversation very easily admiring the new auto. He told her that his pickup truck was parked a few blocks south of the deli out of gas and he asked her if she knew where the closest gas station was that would be open at that late hour of the night.

She told him where there was one and volunteered to drive him to the station adding that it was on her way home.

After he got in the car and away from the deli he threatened her with a knife he always carried with him, although he had never used it for anything in the past except to open paint cans.

He had her drive them to a wooded area East of Seaford where he attempted to rape her, but she begged him not to do it because she was pregnant, and she offered him oral sex if he did not rape her. He had never had oral sex before and decided that he would accept her offer.

Afterwards he became afraid that she would tell on him for trying to rape her and with his hands strangled her to death. Who needed a wife he thought to himself. He didn't need Jennifer. He had killed his first victim and enjoyed doing so.

He then drove Harriet's car to Laurel, his home town, and parked it in a church parking lot where he wiped the car clear of finger prints. After taking her money out of her purse, he placed the purse and its' contents on the front seat with other items to make it look like a robbery. He then walked the two blocks to the apartment he shared with a friend.

The next morning, after her body was found, the newspaper carried a story about Harriet's death and an interview with one of Harriet's friends who mentioned to the reporter that Harriet's best friend, Jeanne Records was reported to be very distraught over Harriet's death as they were rarely seen without being together. They had been close friends since school days. Jeanne also mentioned that the class was to hold a reunion at the Flagship restaurant and they would all miss her classmate not being there.

Jeanne told the reporter she had left Harriet at a baby shower they had both attended the very evening that Harriet disappeared.

Fred heard her comments on the TV that evening and decided that he would put Jeanne to rest just as he had done with Harriet. He had a strange urge that he just had to rape this friend of Harriet's.

The TV reporter stated in his commentary that she worked at the Flagship Restaurant where Jennifer worked and he went there and waited in the parking lot until the reunion was ended. He did not go in the restaurant for fear that Jennifer would see him.

Using the picture in the newspaper and his memory of her appearance when she was on the TV news program he identified Jeanne as she left the party, he watched as she got in her car. She was alone. He followed her and when she parked the car at a restaurant he followed her and got out of his pickup truck after parking next to her, and struck her on the head with a crow bar.

He quickly loaded her in his pickup truck and took her to the same wooded area just off the Nanticoke River locally referred to as 'The Island' where he had taken Harriet just a few days earlier.

Unlike Harriet, Jeanne put up a fierce struggle with him and Fred found himself enjoying the struggle. He used another length of wire that he had cut from a roll of wire he had stolen from the truck he had driven to a paint store four days earlier.

He then went to his apartment in Laurel, packed his few possessions, and told his roommate the next morning that he was going south to find a steady job. He had given up on Jennifer.

He spent that evening in North Carolina. He had left Seaford without making another attempt to convince Jennifer to go with him. He had decided that marriage was not for him, but he still could not get her out of his mind.

He would come back to Delaware after he got a steady job and then try again to get her to go to Florida with him.

CHAPTER THREE

FOLLOWING A LOVELY HONEYMOON VACATION in Aruba, Bill and Helen returned to Delaware and were busy looking for a new home and furniture. Their son Douglas was enrolled in the same preschool as Bob and Kathy's son Norman. Their daughter Nancy was enrolled in the first grade in the Newark Elementary school.

Three months had passed and the new family was now settled in their new home in Stanton, Delaware not far from their friends Bob and Kathy.

Bill was settled into his new job as head of the FBI's branch office in Wilmington and Helen was very pleased with her job working with children of New Castle, Delaware with learning disabilities for which she had been trained; but she soon discovered that she would soon have to take a leave of absence because she was now pregnant with Bill's first child.

She called her friend Kathy to tell her about her pregnancy and Kathy told her, "Oh I am so happy to hear that, but guess what?"

"What's that Kathy?"

"I'm pregnant too. Bob and I are both ecstatic about it. I bet that Bill is as pleased as we are."

"Yes he sure is; but he does love my two as if they were his own. We are in the process of having their last names changed and he wants to start the process for their adoption as well. How far gone are you? I'm due in November."

"I'm due in late September. I think I will talk to Bob about doing those two things with Norman. It sure will eliminate a lot of queries as they get older."

"Yes, that is why Bill and I decided to do it. Why don't you all come over for a cookout Saturday afternoon? We can celebrate our pregnancies and I know the kids will love it, the food that is."

"That's sounds great to me. I'll ask Bob as soon as he gets home, but I am certain that he will agree. What do you want me to bring?"

"Nothing at all, I went shopping yesterday evening and I have everything we will need, hamburger, hot dogs, rolls, and lots of beer for Bob and Bill."

"How about if I bring over a few ears of corn, I just got some Florida white corn, and it's delicious. I have a big pot to boil it in and I'll bring that too."

"Great, I'll see you all then. How about three o'clock? If Bob can't make it, I'll call you as soon as he gets home."

"Three o'clock will be perfect."

Bob and Kathy arrived promptly at three and Bill was already setting up the outdoor grill for cooking the meat. In a few minutes all was well underway, and the men sat back with a beer and were watching the progress of the burgers and franks and the children playing with the neighbor's dog. The women were cooking the corn in the house.

"Bill, Kathy told me that you were to be a father."

"Yes Bob and I understand you are too."

"Yes that's right. It must have been something in the water."

"Yeah, I guess that was it. I'm really pleased about it."

"Yes, I am too, I'm going to try and talk Helen into going back to Seaford when it comes time for her to give birth, so she can be near both her mother and her mother-in-law. My mother is in Tennessee and my dad is ill so her help is out of the question."

"Helen's in-laws now live in her old house down there. You remember that one don't you? You were with me several times when I went to see Helen there. It has lots of room for visitors. Helen is determined that her children stay in close contact with their grandparents and uncles, and I agree. All of our children will grow up with three sets of grandparents."

"Well, Norm has already become my mother's grandson, and all is okay on that score. I am sure that Kathy will be under my mother's wing during this pregnancy. She is as excited about it as Kathy and I are. This will be her second grandchild. She has Norman calling her 'granny' already."

"Has Helen finally agreed with the findings and conclusion that Horace was the murderer of Jeanne and Harriet? I know that you told me she was not convinced at the time of his having done those things."

"No she hasn't come to terms with it; but I fear that is partially because of the fact that she doesn't want her children to be known as children of a murderer. She still tells me that she just knows Horace could not have done it. Yet, everyone in Seaford involved with the case, including myself, felt that he did it to keep from losing a lot of money in the divorce settlement; but now that I look into the matter, I am convinced that there is a possibility that she may be right."

"I know now, that if the case had gone to trial, he would not have been found guilty on what little evidence we had. His guilt was decided solely by the wire found in his old pickup truck. If there had been a jury trial, I think they would not have accepted that as proof without reasonable doubt, as they call it, because anyone could have put that wire in his truck."

"But Bill, what about his calling his farm manager to come get him in Laurel that night and Harriet's car being found in Laurel, and of course his farm helper saying that he had seen her car parked many times in back of his poultry buildings?"

"And that Bob is the only thing that keeps me from agreeing with Helen on the possibility of his innocence. I just don't have any idea that would eliminate that item as evidence of his guilt."

"What about the DNA report—wasn't that determined to be his?"

"Bob, there is no argument at all that Horace was having sex with both girls, but that does not make him their murderer. If he was having consensual sex with both of them why did he have to rape and kill either one of them?"

Kathy and Helen brought out of the house items to place on the outdoor picnic table. Kathy asked, "Hey guys how are the burgers and franks coming? We are all done in the house and will have everything on the picnic table shortly."

"Bring it on Kathy we are ready with the burgers. Hey you kids, are you ready for something to eat?"

"Yeah, I want a hotdog, come on Doug and Nancy, let's go eat."

Chapter Four

FRED MESSICK WAS HONESTLY TRYING to quit his raping and killing. He had tried several times but he always found himself back on a search for of a young woman to rape and kill.

After every rape and murder he soon found himself staging his victims in sexually explicit positions and taking their pictures. He got pleasure in reviewing the photos and was making attempts to stage his victims in different positions. His collection of pictures was growing and when he looked at them he was always aroused.

But, immediately after every rape and murder he found himself in a period of remorse and each period of remorse was staying with him for longer periods of time.

Jennifer was still on his mind. He was having dreams of their being married and making love. He decided that if he had married Jennifer, he would not have found himself in such a mental state. He decided he would go up to Delaware and see if he could talk her into coming to Florida with him once again. She had refused him before because he did not have a job but he now had a permanent position with one of Tampa's largest contractors.

He was convinced that only by a marriage to Jennifer would he be able to stop his idiotic urge to rape. He just had to go to Delaware and get her. It would soon be too late.

He had never raped her when they were dating. He loved her like no other woman he had ever dated. Truly he would have made love with Jennifer if she was willing; but he had no desire to force himself on her and strangely he was willing to wait for marriage. She wanted that and his love for her always led him to wait.

He had vacation time and had made up his mind to go to Laurel in the month of December and locate Jennifer. He would give her the engagement ring that he had taken back from her the previous year.

He was still receiving the weekly newspaper and enjoyed reading about the people he knew and news of the area. One column that he always read was called What, Where, Why, Who, and When.

This column existed mostly as a place to report on the residents of Laurel. It was in the last issue of November that he read about Jennifer. It reported that she was a graduate of Laurel High School, who now lived in Seaford and was an employee of the Flagship restaurant. It stated that she was engaged to marry a Bridgeville boy named Richard Bennett who was employed by an oil company in Alaska. No date had been set for the wedding.

It was that news article that upset Fred. He had to contact Jennifer to see if she could be convinced to marry him. He now had a job and could offer her the security that she had demanded before. He was certain that she still loved him. He needed her to quit his raping.

He read again, no date had been set for her marriage. He was convinced that their marriage would put an end to his impulse to attack young women. He would try anything to rid himself of that impulse and he did still love Jennifer.

He asked his employer to move up his vacation time to the following two weeks, telling his employer that there had been a death in his family. His request was approved and Fred left for Laurel, Delaware the next morning after making arrangements for a motel room in Seaford, Delaware.

When he arrived in Seaford he met Jennifer where she was still working, at the Flagship restaurant. She was on duty behind the bar.

He tried to talk to her there; but another bar patron kept hitting on her. Fred tried to get her attention but that patron kept telling him to get lost and stop interrupting his conversation with Jennifer.

Fred and the other man had a few nasty remarks, but the other man was much bigger than Fred and Fred knew he was no match for him, so he left the bar after the bar manager broke up the argument and asked Fred to leave.

It was near midnight and he knew that she used to get off work after one in the morning so, he waited in his motel room until shortly after one o'clock and called her on her cell phone.

He still had her number on his cell phone and when she answered his call, he was able to talk her into meeting him at the parking lot at the hospital in Seaford.

Reluctantly, she met him at the lot and he got out of his pickup truck and got in her car with her. They talked for well over an hour but she would not agree to break her engagement with her fiancé who was in Alaska.

She told him several times that it was late and that she was tired. She finally asked him to get out of her car. He stopped pleading with her and realized that he was fighting a losing battle. For the first time with her, he immediately developed an urge to rape her and have the sex that she had always denied him.

After he raped and choked her to death using a piece of the same wire that he used on his earlier victims he took her body to 'The Island' in his pickup truck, to make it look like she had been killed there. He drove back to his room in the Motel where he packed his bags in preparation for his trip back to Florida.

CHAPTER FIVE

I T HAD BEEN FIVE MONTHS since Kathy and Helen told each other of their pregnancies. They were now in their seventh and ninth months of pregnancy. Kathy was expecting her child any day now.

Bill received a call at his office in Wilmington from Chief Daley of the Seaford, Delaware Police Department.

"Mr. Carle, I hate to tell you this; but we have just found the body of another young woman who was raped and murdered here in Seaford. It has all the appearances of being done by the same person as those two of last year."

"She was strangled in the same manner as the women were last year, in which you were involved here in Seaford."

"We are concerned that this murder may be connected to those murders. The victim was also found very near where those two other ladies in our earlier case were found. Is there a possibility that Mr. Hastings may not have been the murderer after all? Could we have a serial killer here in Sussex County after all?"

"Chief, we were all in agreement after we found that roll of wire in Mr. Hastings's truck last year and those other items; but I am certainly interested in reopening that case. If you are willing, our office will again be happy to assist you with this new case. Based on what you have just told me you just might indeed have a serial rapist and killer in your area after all. Would you like us to assist you?"

"Yes, Bill that is why I called you, I am again asking for your help, and in view of your wife's connection to that former case, Jack Truitt and I were certain that you would want to help us get this matter resolved once and for all—especially for Helen's sake."

"I appreciate that Chief, and yes we will join you to bring this matter to a conclusion not just because of Helen's connection, but because it does look like we do have a serial murderer as you suggested."

"I will assign Bob Spedden to your office immediately, and I will personally accompany him down to Seaford to see you and your staff on Friday morning if that is okay with you?"

"Yes Bill that would be great. It will be nice seeing you guys again. Jack told me just yesterday that he remembered how Mrs. Hastings was arguing with him that she was not convinced her husband Horace had committed the murders."

"Yes, that's true. She argued with me too that anyone could have placed that wire and the gloves in his pickup.

Maybe she was right after all. She even said that she never knew Horace to have worn gloves even in his work."

"Bill I will pull all the files on the former case and have them ready for you when you get here and I will fax the transcripts we have on this new case by mid afternoon so you can see where we are to date. That may help you in making plans for the investigation. I presume that you still have copies of what was obtained during the prior cases."

"Yes we have all of that, so all we will need is what you have obtained recently on this new case that you said you were going to fax. I would imagine that it will be late in the afternoon before we get to Seaford but I will contact you enroute."

That evening at dinner, Bill told Helen, the details of what he had been told by Chief Daley and that his office would be reopening the case.

"I will be sending Bob Spedden to head up the investigation. I told Chief Daley that Bob and I would be going down to Seaford on Friday morning and that Bob would be handling the case. Perhaps you and I could drive down Thursday evening to visit your parents and in-laws and to tell them that the case against Horace was being reopened. I know they will be glad to hear that. We could come back to Wilmington on Friday evening, Saturday, or Sunday."

"Oh, that's wonderful news, Bill. I hope that all of this will clear Horace's name for the sake of the children. I know the Hastings' will be thrilled to hear this, and I will be so happy to visit with them. Please let's stay until Sunday, I am anxious to see them all again. We can stay at my old house where the Hastings' live now."

"I am sure that Kathy would agree to take care of the children on Friday; unless we can take them out of school on Friday and take them with us, but Kathy is so near term I don't want to ask her."

"I guess that's right, why don't we just take them down there with us? I am sure both their grandmother Hastings and your patents would love to see the children anyway. They would only miss school for one day."

"I was going to suggest that you go there when it is closer to the time for the baby to be born and I was hoping you could stay with them for a period of time until you felt you were ready to come home."

"Yes, that would be no problem. I was hoping you would agree to my doing that. I will call Mrs. Hastings and my mother to see if that suits them for the weekend and for me to stay later. I know that my parents would welcome me also. I can make plans for that while we are down there."

CHAPTER SIX

AGENT ROBERT SPEDDEN ARRIVED IN Seaford Thursday evening and reported to the Seaford Police station at eight o'clock on Friday morning as previously arranged.

He advised Chief Daley that the FBI Bureau chief, William Carle, would arrive at about nine o'clock and that Bill would like an audience with the department's team assigned to the murder of this young lady.

"In the meantime, I have read your report, and have several questions that perhaps you can clear up for me. Was the young lady a member of the class of 1984 graduating class like those murdered last year?"

"No, we found no connection. Her name is Jennifer Collins. She was 24 years of age, unmarried, and was an employee of the Flagship Restaurant in Seaford along the waters of the Nanticoke River. She graduated from the Laurel High School in the class of 1985."

"Does she have any connection with anyone mentioned in the case of last year's murders?"

"Not as far as we know; but we have determined that she has worked at the Flagship since she graduated from high school so she was working at the Flagship at the time of those murders. She started working as a waitress in the restaurant but went in the bar to work after she became 21 years of age. You will remember that the Flagship itself was mentioned many times in the prior cases."

"The coroner's report states that she was strangled in the same manner as the earlier victims. Does the report include a description of what was used to strangle her? I am anxious to know if was a wire or a cable and if it matches that cable found on the earlier victims?"

"Yes, it has been determined that the wire found on the victim's neck was identical to that found on Jeanne Records' body and it was one identical to the wire we found in Horace Hastings' pickup truck in the prior case."

"Well that would surely help us in eliminating Horace as the killer of the other two girls doesn't it? Bill and his wife will be happy to hear that."

"At this point Bob, I would suspect that Horace was not the killer as we had thought and the evidence which caused us to think he was the killer is now suspect isn't it? But then there is still a possibility that someone else may have used an identical piece of that wire although I find that hard to believe."

"Yes Chief, I guess we are back to square one again. My thought at the moment lets me think we do have a serial killer on our hands. He may still be here in the area and that is why Bill wants to talk to the team."

When Special agent Bill Carle arrived promptly at nine o'clock, the entire team was already assembled. After the Chief introduced all the FBI agents, agent Carle was given the floor.

"Men and lady, first I want to tell you why we are interested in this case again. Last year we were down here because there were three murders and we always get involved any time there are three or more murders in a nearby area. That is when the term serial rapist or serial killer comes into play and that is when we of the FBI get involved. We backed away from your case last year after we proved that one of your murders was not committed by the same individual."

"Now that we know there have been three murders by the same individual, we are entering the picture again and your chief has agreed to our assistance. The first thing all of you need to understand is just what determines someone to be rated as a serial killer."

"We must know the kind of man we are looking for and what to expect from him. We have a considerable amount of data that we find is helpful in tracking and arresting these types of individuals."

"We need to understand the difference between a man who rapes a girl on the spur of a moment and a serial rapist. First, a serial rapist is one who rapes girls on his constant urge or need to rape simply for the thrill of it. He thinks he can get away with it. Second, In this case we are not talking about a spree rapist or a spree killer or even a mass murderer for that matter. The spree or mass rapist rapes a number of girls and suddenly quits. We have here both a rapist and a killer. He rapes and then kills his victims."

"We from the FBI are here today because we think a serial rapist who also happens to be a serial killer is our suspect in your murders. We also feel that he is not a classmate as we suspected last year, so we will not be redoing all that we did last year."

"It will help you to know what prompts a serial rapist top do what he does. We in the FBI have been collecting data on them for many years, so we can predict their every move, predict where to look for them and predict what to look for in developing a list of suspects."

"From 1984 to 1986, FBI special agents assigned to the National Center for the Analysis of Violent Crime (NCAVC) interviewed 41 men who were responsible for raping 837 victims. That's an average of over twenty rapes per man. An article they published, describes the behavior of these serial rapists during and following the commission of their sexual assaults. The information presented is applicable only to the men interviewed; it was not intended to be generalized to all men who rape. I suggest that all of you get on your computers and Google the report issued by NCAVC on Serial Rapists. You will find some very interesting facts about a serial rapist and those characteristics just may help us find our rapist and killer."

"Now where do we start? A serial rapist/killer, as typically defined, is an individual who has raped and murdered three or more people over a period of about a month, with some down time that we refer to as 'a cooling off period' between the rapes and murders, and whose motivation for killing is usually based on psychological gratification."

"We have had two rapes and murders and now have our third, although the third was not in near term, as I just mentioned, but we cannot be certain that there may not have been others out of our location of which we are presently unaware. ASt this time we don't know what he has done elsewhere. If our statistics are correct we will probably learn that there have been other victims in other areas, and we are approaching this case with that in mind. We will start by trying to connect rapes and murders with similarities to yours."

"The cable used pretty much confirms that we do have a third victim and he may have just come off his so called cooling period."

"Often a sexual element is involved with the killings, but our experts in the FBI state that motives for a serial rapist or murderer include 'anger, thrill, financial gain, and attention seeking'. The rape and murders may all have been attempted or accomplished in a similar fashion and the victims may have had something in common to which the rapist is attracted, for example, all the victims are in an occupation group, or of a particular race, or of a like appearance, sex, or age group. Things like that."

"From what I have read, our victims were all attractive girls, with dark hair, and of the same age group. So we have that to start with."

"Serial killers are not the same as mass murderers nor are they spree killers, who commit murders in two or more locations with virtually no break in between."

"I will ask all your team members to go over all the old transcripts to see if we have missed something. Look for similarities in the victims, the settings, the estimated times of the rape or killing, anything that will establish an MO. I think that we should approach all these murders with that in mind—have we have missed something? I am confident there is reason these women were raped and killed other than a need for sex."

"Using the killer's modus operandi, or MO, we hope to track this guy. We know now that he does use a certain wire cable to strangle his victims, and so far the victims all fall into about the same age bracket. They were all young women in their early 20's. We have a start on arriving at his MO and I am sure that will eventually lead us to him."

"I still ask myself, why he uses that wire. Certainly a rope would be much easier to use. I asked the experts at headquarters just this morning and they said that perhaps the killer wanted us to know that they were all his victims, and that was what he had on hand when he did his first killing. Credit for his rapes and murders is often a trait of a serial killer."

"There are some other things that I should mention now that may or may not help us. One is that in 70% of our bureau cases, the victims are strangers to the killer. Another fact is that a rapist rarely kills for money, only 19% of all our past cases had money involved, but one of your cases last year did have a theft of money from her purse, but as I recall, it was pretty much established by your detectives, that the money was taken to let us think it was a simple robbery."

Detective Truitt broke in, "Yes, that was Harriet O'Brien, her purse and contents were placed on the front seat of her automobile which was parked in Laurel in a manner that indicated he wanted us to believe it was a robbery."

"Yes we have that all on file. Another characteristic of a serial killer is that they almost all periodically stop killing for periods of time and then restart later usually at a different location. We call this a 'cooling off period'. I feel that he is just coming off a cooling period. I suspect that between the murders last year here in Seaford, and the time of this new murder again in Seaford, that there was probably a series of rapes at other locations and we are checking up on that already."

"It is rare for a serial rapist or killer to have an accomplice, but there have been some serial killers that did work together, and lastly, the intelligence range of rapists is from idiots to very high IQ, so that includes everyone."

"One of the first things we need to do, is to determine just how this serial rapist/killer approaches the women he intends to rape."

"Our studies indicate that there are three different styles of approach. The 'Con approach' is where the killer misleads the victims into thinking that he is someone of authority, a policeman, a fireman, etc."

"Then there is a 'Blitz approach' where the killer uses physical force to subdue his victim and then lastly there is a 'Surprise approach' where the killer watches his victim, like a 'peeping tom' for example, and learns the routine of his victim. He then makes his move when he feels the victim does not expect him to come where she is."

"From what I have heard and read so far, I can't determine for certain if the girls were victims of the Con approach or if they were victims of a Blitz approach. Jeanne Records had evidence of injury which definitely would indicate a Blitz, but we really don't have proof of that yet."

"Just how they were approached and placed into a vehicle with the killer is still unknown."

"A few years back, you may remember the case where a serial rapist and killer named Ted Bundy was killing young girls across the country. He often pretended he needed help in loading something in a car."

"Several times he had his arm in a sling or in a fake cast to get a victim to help him load some items in his car. Then when they came to help him he hit the girls with a crow bar and threw the girls in his car."

"Serial rapists are creatures of habit. What works for them once is most often repeated. I might add that the Con approach was used in 41% of all rapists' first rapes; but a lesser percentage in their subsequent rapes. 23% of all rapes were used with a Blitz approach and 54% of all the cases were of the Surprise approach."

"The vast majority of serial rapists use the Surprise approach because they fear they may not be able to subdue the victim by physical threats or subterfuge."

"Surprisingly the vast majority of rapists use bindings located at the scene of the rape, but a few, like in your case here in Seaford, bring a binding with them such as precut lengths of wire or rope, adhesive tape, or even handcuffs. Several rapists stated that they used the binding to immobilize their victim in performing the rape and then used it to strangle the girl after the rape. I suspect that may be what our killer is doing."

"Rapists maintain control over their victims depending upon two factors, their motivation for the sex attack and or the passivity of the victim. However there are some rapists that rape their victims after they have killed them."

"The vast majority of rape victims are subject to minimal physical force with the amount of force employed more for threats than to punish. We have had many reports that the rapist threatened his victims with disfigurement of their faces if they resisted him and the victims allowed the rape to avoid such disfigurement."

"I think that your rapist uses that special wire or cable to let us know that the victim was his. As I stated earlier that was also the opinion of our experts. They said, and I agree, that a rope would certainly be easier to use. Most rapists want the feeling of power and want credit for their misdeeds. Rapes and killings become like a game to them.

They don't want to be caught but they do want credit for the rape or killing."

CHAPTER SEVEN

"**N**OW BACK TO YOUR NEW victim Chief, have you established where this new victim, Jennifer Collins was last seen?"

"Bill as far as we have determined, the last persons to see her were her fellow employees at the Flagship restaurant. The manager and the employees say that she left work early Friday morning at 1:00 am when the restaurant and bar closed. That was her usual departure time."

"No one mentioned that they actually saw her leave; but her automobile was found parked in the Nanticoke Memorial Hospital parking lot here in Seaford. There were no fingerprints but hers in the car and there were none of her prints on the steering wheel or door handles which may indicate that someone may have wiped the prints off; otherwise there should have been some prints on the steering wheel."

"Evidently she was alone from the restaurant after she completed her evening of work. Why she went to the hospital is unknown and we are quite certain that she did not visit anyone there because it was after one o'clock in the morning when she left work. We feel that perhaps she went there to meet someone."

"None of the Flagship employees remembered having seen her talking with anyone before leaving the restaurant and none saw her leave with anyone."

"Who reported her missing? The report states that she lived in an apartment with a roommate named Ethel Smoot who lives in Blades, Delaware."

"Yes that is correct. The town of Blades is directly across the Nanticoke River on old Highway 13 to Laurel. You cross the river and you are in the other town. We got a report on Saturday the second of January, from her mother, Mildred Collins, who lives in Laurel. Her mother called us after she had been contacted by the manager of the Flagship restaurant when she didn't report for work last Friday night and after her roommate Ethel had told her Jennifer did not come home after work last Thursday night."

"That call was made to us two days before her body was found last Sunday on the 5th of January."

"Did she have any male friends? If so, have they been questioned about their last having seen her? Or have they been asked to account for their activities over the week of the murder?"

"Yes, we have that all well under way. Her roommate, Ethel Smoot, told us that Jennifer used to date a man from Laurel, but she broke up with him. She was not dating other men anymore because she was engaged to be married to a boy working in Alaska as soon as he got home from Alaska in January."

"Miss Smoot did not know all the names of the men that had dated her in the past; but she did give us a list of three names that have not yet been interviewed pending a background check on them has been completed."

"We have been investigating their backgrounds and we are quite certain that none of them are involved. We will be interviewing them individually as soon as we complete establishing all we can learn about the victim."

"Like I just mentioned, Miss Smoot did say Jennifer had been engaged once before to a man from Laurel, but we were told that she had broken off their engagement well over a year ago and he moved somewhere down south. He does not live in the area at this time. She thought he might live in Florida."

"Did you get the name and address of that individual? Past suitors are always a prime suspect."

"Yes and no. Yes, his name is Fred Messick, a former native of Laurel and we found that he graduated from the Laurel High School in 1983. We also found that he lived for a short time in an apartment building in Laurel, Delaware across the street from the post office building. He was reported to have moved to Florida or somewhere in the south about a year ago and no, we do not know where he is now or where he moved but we were told that he left Laurel after he and Jennifer broke up. He last lived in Laurel in 1989. He left Laurel without telling his roommate exactly where he was going or why he was leaving. But his roommate did tell us that Fred was not getting enough work in the area and was going south to Florida where they could work all year and where there was a lot of work available at union wages."

"His former roommate, George Hearn, told us that Fred was not married and was a self employed house painter. George is also a house painter and he said they often worked together on some jobs when Fred was in Delaware."

"Did you get any information on why he and Jennifer had broken off their engagement or if they were dating again?"

"Yes, we did ask Mr. Hearn about that, and he said that he thought he may have gone to Florida to get a steady job with a big constructing company in the Tampa Bay area. We asked him why he left the area without Jennifer and he said that Fred had asked her to go with him and she refused because he did not have a job lined up down there. He claimed that Fred was very upset about that."

"Mr. Hearn told us that he had not seen or heard from Fred since he left Laurel over a year ago. Mr. Hearn did say that he had seen Jennifer at the Flagship several months ago, and that when he asked Jennifer if she had heard from Fred. She told him that she had not seen or heard from him since he left Laurel and that she was now dating a new guy from Bridgeville that worked in Alaska, and that she was going to marry him after the New Year when he came home."

Chief Daley told everyone in the room that he had setup a meeting of all personnel in the conference room in thirty minutes and asked them to bring all members of their individual teams to join him in the conference room at that time. He said it would be a brain storm type meeting to get them all going in the same direction.

At the start of the meeting the Chief arranged to introduce the two FBI agents Milligan and Spedden who were still in the building. After introducing everyone who was heading up a special team in attendance, Chief Daley proceeded with the introduction of special agent Carle who then took the podium.

"Men, I am pleased to see you all once again, but sorry that we meet again under such circumstances. I am sure that Chief Daley has told you that Robert Spedden has been assigned to assist you in not only this case but that he is also under an instruction to determine if this murder and rape is connected in any way with the murders and rapes we thought we had resolved last year. A few minutes ago we had a meeting with the individuals that your chief has appointed to head up the various teams that you are all assigned to. I just wanted to let you all know that we of the FBI are here to assist you in your endeavor and to answer any questions you may have on how we will proceed."

"We have nothing concrete at this time to indicate any connection to last year's murders, except the Coroner has advised us that the wire used to kill this new victim, Jennifer Collins, was identical to the wire used to kill Jeanne Records and possibly Harriet O'Brien last year."

"We are very concerned about that, and that does suggest a possible connection that we will follow up on."

"As you know the case last year never went to a jury trial because Horace Hastings, who was determined to have killed the two girls, was himself killed by another man not involved with the murder of the two ladies."

"The prosecutor, if you will recall, simply closed the case because there was no one to bring to trial. Horace was dead."

"I read just last week about a jury trial of a mother in Kentucky accused of killing her little two year old daughter who was found not guilty by the jury in spite of a lot of evidence that seemed to point to the mother as the killer."

"That jury was not convinced that the evidence presented to them, was positively proven and they felt there was a reasonable doubt that she had actually killed the child. The public was very upset at the jury's verdict, because the media had certainly convinced the public that she was guilty and many individuals accused the jury members of not doing the job they were instructed to do."

"But the jury did in fact do their job. And that job was to find the defendant guilty or innocent if, and I repeat if, guilty or innocent beyond any reasonable doubt."

"After they found the mother not guilty, several of the jurists were threatened with physical harm and because of that, we were called in to protect those jurists and to arrest those making the threats against them."

"I might add that at a later date, that mother was actually proven innocent. So I hope you understand why it is not only important but necessary for the prosecutor of a case to prove his case to the point that there is no reasonable doubt. Just imagine if that mother had been found guilty and sentenced to death."

"That is the very reason that the state prosecutor closed our case last year. We felt that the evidence we did have against Horace Hastings appeared to be all we needed; but he was not convinced that the evidence was proof positive and because Mr. Hastings was dead there was nothing to lose on closing the case."

"If the Coroner is right, then if Horace had not been killed, we possibly may have sent to trial an innocent man. We must have proof without any doubt that our suspect in this case is guilty. So I ask you to prove, and prove again what you are told, what you suspect, and what the evidence indicates."

"If what I see here today is correct, the prosecutor made a wise decision in not going to trial last year. So here we are, with the murderer of three women on our hands."

"The killer now meets all the FBI qualifications to be called a serial killer and we must get this person and get him soon."

"I mention this story about the mother accused of killing her baby only because the jury did in fact do their job correctly, by finding the mother not guilty; because in their opinion the evidence presented was not proven beyond a reasonable doubt, and as it turned out they were right. The system does work."

"If you will review the testimony that was presented in your case last year, there are two things that I have since thought just might have not been proven without a reasonable doubt."

"The first item was that the wire and the work gloves with blood on them found in Horace's old pickup truck do not prove that he put them there. Wouldn't you think that he would have discarded them someplace else rather than in plain sight in his own truck?"

"That question now makes me think, that perhaps and just perhaps, they may have been placed there by someone just to implicate Horace."

"The other item I now question, is that we were convinced that the semen DNA we found on both girls was reported to have been from Horace and that, with the wire, let us all believe that Horace was the killer. But it was also proven, and well documented, that Horace was indeed having sex with both the ladies. Therefore the fact that his DNA was found on both girls, does not prove that he murdered them. It merely says that he did have sex with the women."

"He had no reason to rape either of them because he had consensual sex with both of them many times before the murders."

"Perhaps Harriet was not actually raped as first reported, but killed for another reason. That may account for the question we had at that time, as to why she was fully dressed when found, with no visible signs of having been raped."

"We now wonder why she was killed if she had not been raped. We need to get an answer to that question. There has to be a reason there somewhere."

"Now with all that said, I am sure you all know that Horace's widow, Helen, and I were married after the case was closed last year."

"Helen and I had been friends for several years during our college years. Helen has insisted that Horace could not have murdered the two women, and she and I both are hoping that Horace can eventually be vindicated of that crime because of the hurt and problems her children will face as children of a murderer."

"I do admit that up until now, and before another murder was committed using a piece of identical wire, I was certain that Horace had committed the crimes. All the evidence gave me that impression; but now, I am thinking that just perhaps, Helen was right when she told us that she knew Horace could not have done that."

"So, now I have a feeling that she was right all along; but at any rate, we now have the task to find the murderer of Miss Collins and I hope that we can determine quickly who that murderer is."

"Because of the identical wire the killer used, our case now has all the ingredients of a serial killer. We must find him quickly before he kills again. The bureau experts say that he will kill again and probably will do that very soon."

"Mr. Carle, I am Henry Fisher, a reporter for the Salisbury Times. Did I understand you correctly that you suspect that we have a serial killer here on the Eastern Shore?"

"Thank you Mr. Fisher, I am not certain that he is now on the Eastern Shore or specifically here in the Seaford area, but it is my personal opinion that the murderer of Miss Collins, may possibly be a serial killer and we will be taking action with that thought in mind."

"Thank you, does that mean that you approach serial murder investigations different from other murders?"

"No, that is not correct. It only means that we expand the area of our search for the killer. We take a look at all unsolved murders, even those out of the area or across the country, that have similarities in evidence, similar MO's or those that may possibly have a connection to each other, in hopes of finding leads, including the case we are currently working on."

"We have considerable data that we put into play when a serial rapist is thought to be the suspect. As an example, we would be very interested in looking into any murders where death was by strangulation with a similar type of wire. That is why we are now of the opinion that the murderer of Miss Collins may well be the same person to have killed the previous two murders. The wire used in all three murders is identical."

"Then am I correct in assuming that there is a possibility that Horace Hastings may not have been the murderer of Harriet O'Brien and Jeanne Records last year. Is my assumption correct?"

"Your assumption is correct; but as I said, that is only a possibility we have not proven that otherwise as of yet."

"You must remember that Horace was not proven guilty by a jury trial. The case was made inactive; but has never been officially closed, because he was dead and because all the evidence at the time did point to him. But as you now know, from what we just mentioned, there is now a question that the evidence used to place the case against Mr. Hastings in an inactive status has now been found questionable."

"Does that mean that you are also reopening the murders of Harriet and Jeanne, those ladies who were killed in last year's so-called Class Reunion Murders?"

"Yes, this new evidence warrants that we again look into those cases. We always consider any and all evidence that ties our cases together—active or inactive."

"Then will you be questioning those same individuals questioned before in those earlier cases, especially those that were in jail at the time? Will they be returned to jail?"

"Mr. Fisher, we do not identify or discuss the steps or actions we will be taking on our ongoing investigations. We do hold weekly press interviews on our activities or whenever we feel we have information that the public should be made aware of. I would hope that you will not put any emphasis on our past cases in your newspaper articles at this time because we can't positively make that connection at this time. If we do get a connection to those old cases I will certainly make you aware of that fact."

"Your question about the suspects that were released from jail being picked up again, will be determined by the prosecuting attorney and of course the judge."

"Chief Daley, I must be back in touch with my office in Wilmington, and before I leave, I would like to meet with all of your investigating team captains as soon as possible, so that we can plan our steps of action on the case at hand."

"Great Mr. Carle, I will have the team leaders available in our conference room at 11:00 this morning if that is okay with you and Mr. Spedden?"

"Yes that would be perfect."

"Okay then so I am closing this meeting so we can all get to work. Thank you all for coming."

CHAPTER EIGHT

A SUB HEADLINE ON THE SALISBURY Times front page the next morning read 'Seaford Class Reunion Murder case reopened. William Carle the FBI agent in charge of the investigations, states that there is a possibility a serial killer could have been the killer of Jennifer Collins as well as the Seaford ladies of last year.'

As the FBI and the team members from the Seaford Police Department got together for their first weekly meeting, Mr. Carle told the chief, "Damn that reporter. I was unaware that we had persons in the room yesterday that were not on our team. I would not have mentioned several items that I did, had I known."

"Luckily, I don't feel that I mentioned anything that will be any serious problem for us. It is important that we keep our activities within our own group so I would appreciate that Agent Spedden or Agent Milligan, be made aware of any such meetings, where the press is in attendance. It is also important that your team keep the plans we undertake private as well."

"Like we did last year, we will on occasion, release information to the press that we feel will assist us. The press at times is very helpful and we often use them to cause something to happen."

"Mr. Carle, I apologize to you for not introducing those persons at the meeting who were from the press."

"There's no harm done Chief, and there is no need to apologize. I just didn't want the killer to know that we had a possible connection to last year's murders just yet. I didn't want the killer to know that, because he might quit using the one thing that ties all the murders to him, and that is his using that cable. That is the only thing that he does that helps us identify those rapes and murders that he is responsible for."

"I didn't do my duty—I should have determined who was in the audience. Perhaps the article will bring to light something that will help us. Now let's get started. Mr. Spedden will outline how we will begin."

"Thank you Bill, well we will certainly start with Jennifer's former fiancé Fred Messick and we will interview any of her former boyfriends. They are always prime suspects."

"We need to know if anyone was seen talking to Jennifer at the Flagship restaurant at any time near the night of her death. We need to know places that Jennifer could have been seen. Who were her close friends? We will have to check her friends at both work and at her place of residence in the town of Blades. I would be very interested to determine if Jennifer knew, or had any contact, with Harriet, Jeanne or Horace."

"We need to do a background check on Fred Messick. Fred was once engaged to Jennifer and had moved somewhere in the South, probably Florida. We need to know exactly when they broke up. When did Fred go to Florida? Was it really Florida? Did he ever return to Laurel? Is he in the area now?"

"We must not allow ourselves to get too deeply involved with any one person. As Bill told us yesterday, a serial rapist and murderer usually keep their victims within a specific group such as prostitutes, a particular age group, a certain ethnic group, etc. They usually do not kill persons well known to them. It becomes like a game to them."

"There is however something that usually triggers their first killing and that is why I am so concerned with this Fred Messick. It just might have been Jennifer's refusal to go south with him that was his trigger; but what gives me real concern, is why he came back to Delaware to kill Jennifer later if in fact; he did kill Harriet and Jeanne."

Detective Jack Truitt said, "Mr. Spedden, I think that the fact that Mr. Messick was reported as having left the area last year about the same time as the death of Harriet and Jeanne, and now we have had another death here, just might indicate that Mr. Messick is back in the area. I would suggest that we make a search for him locally and do it soon."

"Excellent, Jack that is the type of thought we need. Mr. Messick is now known to have left the area about the time of the first murders a year ago, and now his old girl friend has been killed. That would indicate to me, as it did Jack, that Fred may be our guy and he may be back in our area."

"Jack, I would like for you to do some digging into his old friends, etc. and maybe we can start by looking for a vehicle at the local motels, bars, etc. that have a Florida or other southern state tag."

"Mr. Spedden, I will start working on that today."

"Great, and Jack please just call me Bob."

"Men I have just asked Jack to take a step in a direction that makes sense in view of what we do know about Mr. Messick, but that is just not what serial killers do. If Mr. Messick is indeed our killer, he has just made his first mistake. Serial killers usually do not kill anyone to whom they can be easily connected. They prefer killing complete strangers to whom they cannot be directly connected. So there is a possibility that he did not kill Jennifer or the other ladies at all."

"With all of that said, we still must find where Fred Messick is right now. We will have him picked up as a suspect. We definitely have enough evidence to do that."

"We also need to interview the employees of the Flagship restaurant again. This time we need to know anything they can tell us about Fred or the victim. Who can they remember as being in the bar or restaurant the last night she worked."

Agent Carle asked, "Has her car been impounded and searched for clues? That should be enough for us to get started. I wish I could be here to work with all of you but unfortunately I will be returning to my office in Wilmington over the weekend. Agent Bob Spedden will be reporting to me daily."

"If Bob deems it necessary, I will send additional agents to help in your work. I have already assigned Agent George Milligan to the case to work with Bob. He and Bob will be here with you until such time as the case is closed. I wish you luck and I want you to know that you will have the full support of the FBI. All of our resources and services are available to your Chief. I am rather sure that I will be back in Seaford several times during the investigation."

Jack Truitt, the Seaford Police Department's head detective, and Agent Spedden made plans to meet the next morning at Jimmy's restaurant at eight o'clock. Bob remembered that he obtained a lot of good leads while having breakfast with the locals on the previous murders.

"Why hello Mr. Spedden, just couldn't stay away from my wonderful breakfasts could you? I'm pleased to see you again. I suppose that our murder last week has brought you back—right?"

"Yes, to both your questions. We do need some help once again. Did you or any of the breakfast gang know the victim Jennifer Collins? Your group was so helpful to us last year we thought it would be a great place for us to start on this new incident."

Jim Elliott, a local barber and one of the regular breakfast gang said, "Yes, I knew her. She worked at the Flagship restaurant. She worked in the bar. She was a very pretty girl and very friendly. She sure made a good drink."

"Do you go to the bar at the Flagship very often?"

"I go to the restaurant almost every other Thursday evening to attend our Lions Club meetings that meet there on Thursdays for dinner. Some of we members usually hang around the bar for a beer after the meeting. That is about the only time I go in the bar."

"Do you recall anyone that was particularly attracted to Jennifer on any of those times you did go in the bar?"

"Well Jennifer was a very friendly young lady and a pretty one at that. Many of the single men were attracted to her. She was always teasing them; but as far as I know, she never seriously returned their offers of her going out with them."

"I have never seen or heard anything that gives me an opinion as to her personal life. As far as I know, she was a very friendly young lady. I can say one thing, she had a clean mouth unlike most bar girls. I have never heard her say a curse word or gossip as so many of the bar maids do."

"I do remember that on one occasion a week or so ago, I don't know the exact date, there were two guys in the bar, both of whom appeared to be flirting with Jennifer and they wound up in a pretty bad argument with each other when one of them tried to get the other man out of his conversation with Jennifer."

"One of them left the bar angrily. But I didn't know either of the men or what the argument was about."

"Then that would probably be on a Thursday if you had been at the Lions Club, Is that correct?"

"Yes, it was definitely on a Thursday night but I am not sure which week it was now. I think it may have been Thursday of last week but it may have been the week before that. Perhaps some of the other guys who were in the bar after the meeting may be able to say which Thursday it was or possibly identify who the men were."

"So you are certain you didn't know who either of these men was? Did you, by chance, hear either of the men or Jennifer, mention any names?"

"No, as I said I didn't know either one of them but I am sure that I have seen the one that left mad around here somewhere; but I just can't recall where. I don't know his name."

"Can you recall any of your fellow Lions club members who were there when you witnessed that argument? Or anyone else that may have witnessed the argument."

"For the life of me I can't, but I am sure that Harry Oliphant, the manager of the Flagship was there. He may be able to help because he came over to them and broke up the argument. He asked the smaller of the two to leave and he did leave angrily. I might add."

"If I were to show you photos of a group of men in the argument at a later time, do you think you could identify the men?"

"I'm sure that I could identify the man who left the bar—I know that I have seen him before; but the other man—maybe I could remember him from a picture; but I'm not sure I could identify him."

"Okay, then you can probably remember some features of the guy that left. Can you describe for us what you did see about him? Did he wear glasses—have a beard—tall or short—those sorts of things?"

"Oh dear let me think. I know he was not wearing glasses and I know he was much shorter than the other man. I would guess that he was no more than 5 feet 6-8 inches, He was a white man, had dark hair, brown as I recall, and oh yes, I remember that he was wearing a jacket which appeared to be a work jacket, denim I think. It had a lot of paint on the sleeves. I bet he was an artist or a painter. He also had a bad scar over his left eye. Yes, I do remember that scar. I remember that because I was thinking that if he didn't quit aggravating the other guy, he would have another one over the other eye."

"Can you describe that scar?"

"Yes. It was horizontal just above the eyebrow and was about an inch or inch and a half long. It was a deep scar that looked like it was not properly taken care of when he got it."

"Well that will give us several things to look for and it may be of enough help to point us in the right direction. I will contact the manager of the restaurant later today.

Should any of you guys think of anything that may help us, please give us a call at the police station."

Henry Mitchell, a local appliance dealer said, "Mr. Spedden, I was talking to Jennifer on one occasion, I can't remember the date or time, but she told me that her boy friend was working on some oil pipe lines in Alaska, and that he was coming home to marry her in January. We were talking about the weather up there in December and I told her I couldn't believe they would have been able to work up there at that time of the year. She said he didn't mind the cold but that the money was great and that he would have enough to get them started."

"Thank you Mr. Mitchell, everything helps. That indicates that he and Jennifer were definitely still on good terms doesn't it".

Bob made a note on his tablet that he should attempt to get a photo of Fred from one of the yearbooks of the graduating classes of the Laurel High School. He was interested to see if he had that scar when he was in high school.

When Jack and Robert got back to the police station, FBI Agent George Milligan, who had been promised by Mr. Carle to help them, had already been briefed on the case by Chief Daley. Agent Carle excused himself and told the chief he would be back in the morning before he left for his office in Wilmington.

CHAPTER NINE

BILL ARRIVED AT THE FARM house to join his wife Helen and the Hastings family for dinner. He confirmed what Helen had already told them—that the murder cases for both Jeanne and Harriet had been reopened, and that there was a possibility Horace may not have committed the murders as was determined earlier.

"Bill, can you tell us what has happened that lets you think that Horace did not do what he was charged with?"

"Mrs. Hastings, I can't go into detail at this time to tell you why the case has been reopened other than to tell you that we have new evidence that appears to prove Horace's innocence."

"I will say, it has to do with the wire that was used to kill this new lady. I do hope you understand the reason I can't elaborate on the details. We just don't want the killer to know everything that we have for fear that he will change his habits. I know that you and your family would not divulge the information that we have; but we make a habit of not revealing information until we are certain that we are right. I know that you understand. If all we know became known by the killer, it might cause him to change his habits or to disappear from our area leaving us exactly as we were before."

"We want him to think that we have closed those earlier cases. So I do hope that all of you will not mention just yet, to anyone, not even your best friends, that Horace has been proven innocent. For your information, as I said earlier. it does have something to do with that wire and everything will eventually be publicized and Horace will be completely cleared."

"Mom, I understand exactly what Bill is telling us. We should not mention to anyone that the case has been reopened or why it was reopened. We surely don't want to do anything that may hinder their investigation to clear his name. We do want Horace vindicated from this case, so let's all keep this matter to ourselves and just pray that Bill's men will eventually prove Horace is innocent without any doubt, and that they will find the person that did do the killings."

"Yes son I agree, and let's all keep the police, Bill, and the FBI men working on the case, in our prayers. I'm going to ask our church to put the family of this new girl on their prayer list. We all know what the family is going through right now don't we?"

"Helen, I am so happy that you are going to be a mother again. We want you to know that child will be welcomed into our family, just as your husband Bill has been."

"Thank you Mrs. Hastings and I want to thank you all for staying with me over this ordeal. It was comforting to me to have had your support. Now, while we are all here together again, how are things working out here on the farm? Is Steve doing okay and reporting to you as he was instructed?"

"Oh yes, Helen he is doing a great job. Since he was given the new Farm Manager position and is now a property owner, thanks to you, you would think he owns the entire farm operation."

"You could not have selected a better man to oversee the farm. He even overlooks the poultry business for the boys. All of us certainly approved of your gifts to him of the old farmhouse, and some land from Horace's estate. It was not only a Christian thing to do, but one that has taken a lot off the backs of Frank and Alan."

Frank said, "Alan and I talked about this just last week and we decided that we would give him a very good bonus as a Christmas gift. Without him we would probably have to hire another hand."

"By the way, Helen, Steve suggested that we sell Horace's old pickup truck. The truck is still titled in Horace's name so, if you want to sell it, you will have to sign the title with your power of attorney."

"Doesn't he or either of you have need or ever use the truck? I don't imagine it has much value."

"No, we don't have any use for it and Steve said that the truck hasn't been used since last year when it was loaned to the guy who painted the roofs on the broiler houses so he could go to town and get some paint."

"Then why don't I just give the truck to Steve to do what he pleases with it. He shouldn't have to use his own pickup to go about duties on the farm."

Alan injected, "I think that's a good idea."

Bill suddenly remembered the conversation at the police station just before he left, about Jack and Bob's report that the man who left the Flagship restaurant, after having an argument with another patron, had paint on his jacket.

Bill interrupted, "Frank, when did Steve tell you that the truck had been loaned to a painter?"

"Just last week when he suggested we should sell the old truck."

"Did he loan the truck to the painter or did Horace make the loan?"

"Gosh, I don't know Bill, but I am sure Steve can tell us. Why do you ask about that?"

"Frank, that truck was impounded by the police last year and I now wonder if it had been loaned before it was impounded, or after that date. It may have a bearing on our case. You said that the truck was loaned to someone, a painter, if that is true, then the truck was used by someone other than Horace, and I wonder if it was used before or after Horace and the two women were killed."

"I don't know, but I think Steve is down in the equipment shed right now, at least he was when you drove up. Would you like to go down and see if he is still there?

"Yes, I am anxious to follow up on that question. Mrs. Hastings, will you excuse Frank, Alan, and I for a few minutes?"

"By all means, Bill, we will hold the dessert for all of you, so do come right back. It should be served while it is still warm."

When the men arrived at the equipment shed, Steve was busy changing the oil in the farm tractor and he looked up to see who was opening the shed doors.

"Steve, you remember Mr. Carle don't you? He is married to Helen, now and is still with the FBI."

"Yes Frank. I sure do. I will never forget him for all he and Miss Helen did for us back then. I'm just sorry that he took Miss Helen and the kids to Wilmington. I sure do miss them. I'm happy to see you again Mr. Carle. I hope Miss Helen is pleased with my work."

"Steve, she is very pleased with your work but that is not why I m here. Frank told me just today that you and he were talking about selling the old Chevy truck. I'm talking about the old truck that was parked in back of the No.2 building which you and I talked about last year—it's the one that was parked there when you went to Laurel to get Horace that night. Do you remember that conversation we had about that incident?"

"Yes, I do. The truck is still there and has not been used since the police brought it back when they got done with it. That's almost a year ago now."

"Yes, Steve, that's the one. Now think carefully, Frank said that you told him that the truck was never used and had not been used since it was last loaned to a painter. Do you recall telling him that?"

"Yes, I do. I don't think we need it anymore and other than when the police took it, it has not been used at all. I do charge the battery every so often. It's a shame to just sit there and rust away. I think it needs to have the tires pumped up too. I'll do that in the morning."

"Good boy Steve, now you said it was loaned to a painter. Who was that painter and just when was it loaned to the painter? Did Horace loan the truck or did you loan the truck?"

"Oh I didn't loan the truck, I couldn't do that. I wasn't the farm manager then. Horace was alive and he loaned it to the man. The painters were spraying the roof on the No.2 building at the time and they thought that they would be running out of paint before they got it finished that day."

"Horace didn't want them to stop painting and because the sprayer motors were on the contractor's own trucks, he knew that if they stopped painting they may not come back right away or the same day. You know how painters are. It doesn't take much to cause them to quit for the day."

"So after the painter told Horace that they would have to stop painting and go get some paint, Horace told the paint contractor that one of his men could go get the paint and he could use his old truck. Horace wanted that building finished that day because a load of chickens were to be removed from the building the next day. He wanted the paint to be dry before they were taken to the processing plants because that raises a lot of dust. He wasn't about to let them stop working."

"Thank you Steve, then that means Horace did loan the truck himself. Do you know for sure, if anyone else ever used that truck after the painter last used it?"

"Not to my knowledge, Mr. Carle. I'm pretty positive that no one else ever used it. I keep the keys to it."

"I do charge the battery every once in awhile like I said, and that is the main reason I want to get rid of it. I just don't like equipment sitting around that isn't used or is not ready to use."

"Thank you Steve that's all I wanted to know. By the way, you can get rid of the truck any time you want or you can keep it for your own use. Mrs. Carle will sign the title over to you right away because she is giving the truck to you. She wants you to have it. You can sell it or keep if for your own use. But be sure to take out any parts you need on the farm if they are still in the truck. As I recall there was a lot of farm tools and stuff in it."

"Yes that was true, but I have already moved most of it from the truck to this equipment shed where it is needed."

"Oh, by the way, Mr. Frank, that full roll of wire in the back of the truck that was bought after the last time we replaced the cable on the feeders in the No. 2 building is gone. I know it will soon be time to replace those cables and when I checked to make sure we had enough cable yesterday, I discovered that the new roll of wire was gone. Did you move or use it? I knew there was not enough cable in that old box to replace the ones on the feeder conveyors and I know that they are going to need to be changed real soon especially on the No. 1 building. We didn't change the cable on that conveyor when we did it on the No. 2 building. We are going to need to find that roll or get a new one soon."

"No Steve, I haven't used it or moved it but I will get a new roll ordered this evening. We sure can't keep them running if the cable breaks and we absolutely must have at least one roll in inventory all the time, in case we have a break. I will order two new rolls."

"Thank you Mr. Steve."

Back in the house, and after eating their dessert, the men retired to living room. Alan asked Bill, "Bill did you get the information that you were looking for?"

"Yes, I did Alan, if you will recall, there was a pair of bloody work gloves found in the pickup along with a piece of wire that had blood on it, as well as a matching partial roll of wire. Steve's comments indicate that Horace himself rarely used that truck."

"Now we know that someone else did have access and did use that truck. So someone else did in fact have access to that roll of wire in the truck. Not only that, but he probably still has a lot of it. Just how much cable is there on the roll?"

"The new rolls each contain 150 feet. We require an unbroken length of 110 feet; so if we did replace only the No. 2 house last year we only had 40 feet left on the partial roll. We use the left over cable on those other conveyors that can be spliced together. So I can only guess the length left on the partial roll but the one that Steve says is missing would have had 150 feet on it. Someone has a lot of wire."

"He sure does. Regarding the painter, we will now follow up on that report for dates etc. Agent Spedden will find out the name of that painter."

"If I recall correctly, we have in our investigation records, the name of the painter who was painting the roof when the murders were committed. I remember someone telling us that he was painting Horace's building."

"But please guys don't mention any of this to anyone. Especially to your mother or Helen, we don't want to get their hopes up until we can prove anything that will clear Horace."

Alan told them. "I know who did the painting for Horace. It was Bill Mitchell. He did all of Horace's painting jobs."

Bill called Bob Spedden on his cell phone, and told him all that he had heard from Steve and asked him to review the old files, and see if he could confirm the name of the painter that worked for Horace and then try to get the name of his employee that actually went to get the paint. He told Bob that Alan said the paint contractor was a man named Bill Mitchell."

Before Bill left, Steve came to the house and asked for Mr. Carle. "Mr. Carle, I took everything out of the truck, but now that part roll of wire is gone too. I know it was there when the police took the truck."

"Yes, Steve that is correct, but the police have that small roll of wire as evidence in the murder cases. Thanks for letting me know though."

CHAPTER TEN

BOB SPEDDEN HAD THE TEAM search the records of the murders of the prior year for any reference to a painter and found in the transcript, a meeting that Jack Truitt and Bill Carle had at Jimmy's restaurant, written when they were asking the restaurant's frequent customers if they had any information on Horace's last breakfast there.

In the transcript, he found that a local painter Bill Mitchell, had mentioned in his reply to Jack Truitt, Seaford's detective that he was painting the No, 2 broiler house roof for Horace and he had talked to him about that the last time Horace was seen at the restaurant.

Bob called Mr. Mitchell and requested a talk with him on the matter. A meeting was set up for noon that same day at Jimmy's restaurant.

"Mr. Mitchell, I hope you still remember me, I am Robert Spedden with the FBI and we are now working with the Seaford Police Department on the murder of a Blades girl that was found raped and murdered a little over a week ago."

"Yes, I remember both you and Mr. Carle both. How is Mr. Carle doing these days? I thought that case was closed last year. I suppose that now you want to know about the murder of the new girl."

"Yes those old cases were closed; but we are now investigating, as you guessed, this new murder, and because of its similarity to the previous two, we are attempting to determine if there could possibility be any connection to those two cases. I called you because when I was going through the transcripts of the former case, I came across some information that you told detective Truitt and agent Carle. You told them that you were painting the roof on one of Horace Hastings' broiler houses at that time. Do you remember that conversation?"

"Well I do remember that I was painting one of his roofs, but I can't recall what I told them about that?"

"At this time, Mr. Mitchell, it is not important that you recall what you said, because all I really would like to know is the answer to several questions that we have a need for."

"I will certainly help you if I can."

"Great, when you were painting that roof, it has been reported that you were running out of paint and that you told Mr. Hastings you would have to stop painting for awhile so you could go get more paint. Mr. Hastings told you that because all your spraying machines were fixed to your own trucks, he would loan you his old pickup if one of your helpers would go get the paint."

"We were told that Horace was anxious to get the job done that day, because they were going to pick up a load of chickens from the house the next day and there was always a lot of dust when they did that. He was trying to keep you painting."

"Yes, I do remember that now and we did go get the paint and finished the job."

"Okay, now the question. Do you remember which of your men took that truck and got the paint?"

"Oh dear, I don't remember that. I know I had two crews working on the building. I was spraying one side of the roof and Harlan Boyce was spraying the other side, but I can't recall the names of the two helpers we had who moved our hoses and kept the paint containers filled with paint. We usually picked up local painters we knew when we had a big jobs like Horace's. Harlan did not go get the paint, I do know that."

"I am rather sure that there would have been no more than two men helping us that day. We use helpers only when needed on rush jobs. Perhaps Harlan may remember. I do feel rather certain that Irvin Williams was most likely one of them. Irvin is usually the first one I call. In fact, he is on one of my jobs today working with Harlan."

"Is it okay if I contact him today and see if he can tell us who drove the truck?"

"Sure thing, I'll drive you over there right now if you wish."

"That would really be helpful, but I will drive you over there if that is okay with you. We are instructed to keep our vehicles with us."

The two men drove to a new house where Mr. Mitchell had a crew painting the exterior trim on a new brick house. Mr. Mitchell summoned the painter Irvin Williams to come talk to him.

"Irvin, this is agent Robert Spedden of the FBI. He has a few questions to ask you."

"The FBI, you got to be kidding. I ain't done anything and I pay my taxes."

"No, Mr. Williams, we are only trying o get a few answers that we have on a case that we were working on from last year. That was when two girls were raped and murdered. We are hoping that you can remember working on Horace Hastings's broiler house roof last year when you were painting for Mr. Mitchell."

"Yes, I remember that job. I was working with Bill, Mr. Mitchell that is, on that roof. Horace was the farmer that was killed wasn't he?"

"Yes, that's the one. So you do remember painting on that roof. Is that true?"

"Yes, that is true in part, I was not painting on the roof, I was tending the spraying machines and moving the hoses so they wouldn't get hung up on anything as Bill moved along the roof spraying. It goes pretty fast with a sprayer and you have to keep the hoses clear when the man spraying moves along the roof."

"Harlan was the one spraying the other side, and we picked up another painter to help him at the Sherwin Williams paint store."

"Yes that is correct. It is that man that we are looking for. Do you know his name or anything about him?"

"Mr. Spedden, we independent painters, always hang around the Sherwin Williams paint store in Seaford when we don't have a job of our own. We often leave a notice with the manager of that store as well at other paint stores that we are free to work."

"Mr. Mitchell always gives me a call on the telephone when he has a job for me and I do appreciate that. He did call me to work for him on that job. I don't know the exact date, but it was a full day's work."

"Bill told me that he needed two men and wondered if I knew of another painter that was available. I told him that at the moment I didn't know of any; but I told him that I would go to the paint store and see if they had any painters looking for work. He agreed and I found one on a list at the Sherwin Williams store."

"I don't remember his telephone number or his name. The store manager made the call for me and I asked him if he wanted a job for the day. I do remember that he was from Laurel. He said that he had experience working with spraying machines, so I told him to meet us at the Sherwin

Williams paint store in Seaford where he had left his name. I did tell him that it was only a day job. He said he needed the money and he would come to Seaford to work the day. He worked with us all day and that was the last I ever heard from him."

"Did he tell you anything about himself?"

"Not that I remember other than the fact that he was going to go to a city, because he could earn union wages in a city. I do remember that he said he was going to leave Laurel because he needed more work and pay than he could get here in Sussex County."

"Did he mention where he was going to look for work?"

"Not that I can remember, all he really said was that he was mad because there was no union work in the area here."

"I think he did say that he was going down south because they could work outside all year down there. Probably Florida; but I really don't remember him saying where in the South"

"M. Mitchell told us that Harlan, his other paint helper that day, told him he was afraid that he didn't have enough paint to finish the day's work and that because the sprayers were running on both of his trucks, the man who owned the broiler houses, Horace Hastings offered to loan him the use of his old pickup to go get more paint and that one of we two helpers could go to the store and get the paint while they kept painting. Then the painting on the roof could continue while one of us went to get the paint."

"Do you remember that Bill? It was the other man who went to get the paint."

"Yes, I remember what you said; but I couldn't recall which of you went for the paint."

"Well it was the new guy. I didn't go get the paint because you told me that you knew that I could handle both machines and you weren't sure the new guy could."

"The new guy knew where the store was and because you weren't sure he could handle two painter's hoses, you told him to go get the paint. I was a little ticked off because when he came back we were almost out of paint, and I know he had stopped somewhere for a beer. I could smell it on him."

"Yes, I remember that now. We were upset that we might have run out of paint before he got back and that would have fouled up our machines for sure. Your right, I remember that now."

"Bill did you pay him by cash or check? Maybe you could check your checkbook to see if you wrote his name on the check."

"Mr. Spedden, I can answer that question for Bill. Mr. Mitchell always pays by check, but this guy wanted cash because he was leaving to go south somewhere the next morning. Bill, you paid him cash and I am certain of that."

"Yes, I remember that now but I am sure I would have put his name in my books. Mr. Spedden do you know the date this all happened?"

"Yes I do, but I will have to call the station to get it. Excuse me for a minute or two, and I will have the date for you."

Bob walked a distance away and called the police station and talked with agent Milligan and obtained the date, it was June 20, 1989. Mr. Mitchell then called his wife and she told him that on that date he paid $67.00 in cash to a Fred Cassidy of Laurel, Delaware.

"Yes, Mr. Spedden I do remember that his name was Fred Cassidy."

Bob thanked them and after taking Bill back to Jimmy's restaurant he then went to Laurel and checked at the post office to see if they had a mail address for Fred Cassidy. No record could be found of anyone named Cassidy. Several painters were questioned and none of them knew a Fred Cassidy. It appeared that perhaps Mr. Mitchell had been given a false name.

A visit at the telephone business office also failed to list any customers with the name of Cassidy, and the Sherwin Williams store was contacted to determine if by chance they kept any records of painter names or phone numbers. They decided that he probably used a cell phone and they could not get those numbers.

A current list of five names was available and there was no Fred Cassidy on the list nor was there any Cassidy's on their mailing list. In fact; there were no names on the list that had a Laurel telephone number. The store manager said that his list was of painters that bought paint from the store and that painters looking for work were on memo pads only and they were destroyed periodically.

CHAPTER ELEVEN

BOB SPEDDEN AND JACK TRUITT made arrangements to interview the employees of the Flagship Restaurant where Jennifer Collins worked at the time of her murder.

The first interviews were with those employees who worked in the bar where she worked. There were two girls and three men who worked in the bar regularly and one man and two women who worked periodically in the bar.

The bar manger reported two additional employees who had worked at the bar within the last six months who no longer worked at the restaurant. Both of those employees had not worked at the restaurant during the last three months or more.

The manager stated that he was unaware of any personnel problems that may have prompted anyone to kill Jennifer. All his employees thought a lot of Jennifer and most of them were older than Jennifer and they all treated her like a little sister.

Madelyn Smoot was the first to be interviewed because she worked with Jennifer most of the time. Both were employed on the last tour from three o'clock pm that ended at one o'clock am.

"Miss Smoot, I am Robert Spedden of the FBI and I am working on the death of your fellow employee Jennifer Collins. I've been assigned to the local murder case and I would like to ask you a few questions that may help us in our investigation."

"Why question me Mr. Spedden? Jenny was my best friend?"

"That is exactly why we want to talk to you because you are the one who normally works with her. We are hoping that you may provide us with information that will assist us in finding out who did this terrible thing."

"Please know that we plan to interview everyone who works in the restaurant who knew Jennifer and you have not been singled out for questioning. Also by law, I must advise you of your rights because your answers may be used against you if needed."

Robert read her rights and proceeded with the interview after Madelyn had acknowledged orally that she had been given her rights.

"Thank you Miss Smoot, the reason that we are questioning everyone in the restaurant is because the murder of Jennifer was evidently committed after she left work last Thursday night, or actually after she left the bar at one o'clock in the morning on Friday."

"Do you have any idea who could have committed this murder, or may have had a reason to want her killed?"

"Mr. Spedden, I understand that she was raped before she was murdered. I think that alone would be the reason she was murdered. She was probably murdered by the man that raped her, and she must have known who he was if he had to kill her after he raped her."

"Yes, that is true; but what we are looking for is who she may have known, dated, or a man who may have been turned down by Jennifer for a date. Things like that. Did she ever reveal to you any men that tried to—how do I say it—hit on her?"

"Mr. Spedden Jennifer was a very attractive girl, and most of the men who frequent the bar regularly all try to make time with her, but most of them do that only to get on the good side of her. Most of them are married anyway; but just last week there was a loud argument between two of our customers."

"One of the two was Herman Pusey. He works in Dover, Delaware but lives in Salisbury, Maryland. I think he works at the air base up there. He stops here every so often because Mr. Oliphant, our manager will accept and cash his government checks."

"He stops to get the check cashed and always has a few drinks at the bar. He always asks Jennifer what time she gets off work, and always tries to make time with her; but Jenny always gave him the same answer 'Go home to your wife and kids'.

He just laughs and keeps right on talking to her. Just last week he was at the bar and making his usual sexist remarks to Jennifer when another man, I don't know who he was came in the bar and sat down near him."

"To my knowledge, I don't recall ever having seen this new guy before. He tried to butt into the conversation with Jennifer and Herman told him to shut up and mind his own business."

"The two then had words and our manager finally came over and broke up the argument. There were no blows, but there surely would have been if the manager had not got involved. The stranger left yelling I have a right to talk to her anytime I want."

"What did he mean by saying that?"

"I don't know what he meant by that. I asked Jenny if she knew him and all she said was 'Yes, I used to date him but he moved away and I haven't seen him since then until tonight' I have no interest in him anymore."

"Was this the night that she last worked?"

"Come to think of it, yes, it was the last night that she worked. Oh no, I'm not positive about that I don't know for sure what day or the date that happened."

"Did she mention his name? Do you know any men that she ever dated?"

"I asked her who the guy was, but a customer got her attention, and it never came up again."

"Miss Smoot, Are you really sure that it wasn't on the last night she worked? You seemed so positive when I first asked you. If you don't want to get involved, you can rest assured that we will not make your testimony public. No one will know what you tell us. Don't you want to have this killer caught?"

"Yes, I do, I'm sorry Mr. Spedden; I'm just scared that if he was her killer, he may look for me. I really don't know his name but Jennifer did say that she used to date him and was once engaged to marry him. The only man that I knew for sure that she dated since I knew her was Richard Bennett but he is in Alaska right now. He works for one of the oil companies up there and they write to each other regularly by email and talk periodically on the cell phone. She told me that they were going to get married as soon as he returned to Seaford."

"Do you know his address?"

"No, I don't but his parents live in Bridgeville. His father's name is Ted Bennett and he is an electrician and does our electrical problems here in the restaurant. I am sure they have a telephone. I wonder if they know that Jenny was raped and murdered. Mr. Oliphant, our manager, can probably give you more information about his father."

"Thank you Miss Smoot, we will be in contact with them. Jenny's mother said that she talked to him about

Jennifer's death right after Jennifer was found. Tell me Miss Smoot, have you seen any strangers hanging around the bar over the past few weeks, especially any that had conversations with Jennifer?"

"None that come to mind Mr. Spedden but I will try to think and if any come to mind I will contact you. Jennifer was a popular bartender and everyone liked her. She was always in conversations with the customers."

"Can you recall if that man in the argument with Herman Pusey ever came back in the restaurant?"

"Not on our shift. I would know him for sure. I didn't like his attitude, and I don't like men who can't hold their liquor."

"Are you saying that he was drinking when he was in the argument?"

"He had only a beer or two before the argument; but he sure got riled up when Herman asked Jennifer if she would like to have dinner with him and she said no way. He evidently came in wanting to talk to Jenny and Herman told him to beat it."

"Thank you Miss Smoot, I may have a few pictures later of some men to show you and see if you recognize any one of them as being this guy. You have been very helpful and I want you to know that we will have the man who killed Jennifer behind bars soon. I will see to it that your testimony will be between you and I."

"I sure hope so. I'll be glad to take a look at your pictures."

Agent Spedden was happy he had the name of one of the men in the argument. He made a note to himself to check with the barber that first told him about the argument. He had told him that he had thought he had seen one of them before.

Bob was wondering if Herman Pusey was that one that he may have recognized as having been seen before. He was upset when the other man tried to talk to Jennifer. Was he really interested in Jennifer? He would have to be questioned. He made a note to himself that Fred Messick, to whom she was once engaged could and was most likely, the other man and that he was already a prime suspect.

Next to be interviewed was the manager of the restaurant, Harry Oliphant, who broke up the argument between the stranger and Herman Pusey.

"Mr. Oliphant, I thank you for allowing us to interview your employees to see if we can determine who killed your employee Jennifer Collins."

"I'm pleased to be of help Mr. Spedden. I am just as anxious as you are to get her murderer. Jennifer was one of my best employees. A very nice girl and I just can't believe that anyone would harm her."

"Do you have any idea of why anyone would kill her?"

"Absolutely not but I do feel that she had to have been raped by someone who knew her. I feel that way because he must have killed her to keep her from her telling who raped her. I think it was a simple rape that ended with her being killed."

"I wonder if the women that were raped and murdered last year were killed by the same man. I still feel that Horace Hastings did not kill those two girls."

"Mr. Oliphant, only one of the women last year was actually raped, and we feel that the real murderer was identified in that case."

"I know that is what everyone says; but I still can't believe that Horace Hastings killed those women. Horace was a close friend of mine, and I think I'm a pretty good judge of a man's character."

"Well I must tell you Mr. Oliphant that we have not ruled out that a serial rapist may have been involved in that case, now that we have had another rape and killing, and we have kept all options open."

"Tell me what you know about Jennifer. Do you know who Jennifer may have been dating? Who she was last seen with and were you still on duty when she last worked?"

"Yes I can tell you what I do know. I always try to be aware of what my employees are doing, their families, etc. Jennifer was a wonderful employee. All our regulars thought a lot of her and were hurt terribly when they learned of her death."

"I gave Jennifer a job six years ago. At the time she had just broken up with a man with whom she was engaged. He moved from the area to find work and he wanted her to go with him, but she refused."

"She was hurt and did no dating for a long time. Then just in the last five or six months she started to date once in awhile and just in the last three or four months or so, did she start dating regularly again."

"She was last dating a local boy who works for an oil company in Alaska. He is in Alaska right now and was in Alaska when Jenny was killed."

"They were to be married when he came home next month. She had already scheduled herself off work for two weeks in January right after the fifteenth."

"The last night she worked, a Thursday night, she left work and had her paycheck with her. The check has not been cashed and I put a stop payment on it."

"That was a good idea Mr. Oliphant. We now have that check in custody. It was in her purse."

"Oh that's great, I will see that her mother gets it."

"That will be taken care of as soon as the judge releases her personal effects."

"That's great. I will remove the stop payment I have on it. Now back to Jennifer. Jenny left the restaurant the same time that I did and I saw her off in her car as I got in mine.

We both usually close up the restaurant. The last words she told me were "Have a good weekend, see you tonight or something like that."

"She doesn't work on Saturdays or Sundays. I really think that she must have stopped somewhere before she went home. I understand that her car was found at the Nanticoke Hospital. Why would she have gone to the hospital at that hour? I think that perhaps the rapist met her there before he raped her; but why would she have stopped at the hospital at that hour for anyone to get to her? She must have known the man."

"Those are the same questions that we are trying to get answers to. Could someone have been in her car when she got in it?"

"If there was, I didn't see anyone, and Jenny must not have seen anyone, because she had her window opened and that is when she spoke to me about seeing me later."

"I thank you for the information Mr. Oliphant."

The other employees were all interviewed and there was no additional information obtained.

The next day, the newspaper reported all the particulars of the murder including the Flagship manager's remark about her leaving so early in the morning and his question where she would have stopped or gone to meet someone at such an hour.

The Chief of Police and agent Spedden were very upset to see that in the paper and thought that the leak had to have come from someone within the police department. The Chief called a meeting of everyone in the department as well as the Mayor himself, to advise them that the leak may have come from within. He added that he was not going to look any further for the leak but he wanted everyone to know that any information regarding anything connected to these investigations was not to be released to anyone, not to family or friends and especially not to the press.

"Chief, that leak came from the Flagship Restaurant. I know that because Harry Oliphant, the manager there called me and told me that you had talked to him and was asking me if we would be talking to any of the employees that were not working yesterday."

"He also said that a reporter from the Salisbury Times had been in the restaurant asking questions. He had told him that he had already been interviewed by the FBI. I am sure that is where the leak was."

"Great, I am pleased to hear that; but my request to keep a tight lid on our actions still goes. I am sorry that I even suspected the leak came from our staff. We just cannot let the killer we are looking for know our every move. Again I offer my apologies to all of you."

In mid afternoon, the police got a call from the owner of a local service station owned by Nathan Janosik that one of his employees, Donald Jenkins, had reported to him after reading the story about Jennifer's murder, that Jennifer had bought gas at the station and she had been in the store to purchase cigarettes and a lottery ticket on that early Friday morning.

He reported that she paid cash for the cigarettes and the lottery ticket but had put the gas on her gasoline credit card. He said he knew who she was and where she worked. He frequented the bar some nights if he was not working the late shift at the station. He did not see anyone with her.

Bob immediately sent detective Jack Truitt to interview the store attendant.

"Donald, your store's owner, Mr. Janosik, told us that you thought you had seen Jennifer Collins while you were working the late shift at his station and gave us permission to talk to you about what you two discussed. My name is Jack Truitt, I am a detective with the Seaford Police Department and I want to confirm that sighting."

"Can you tell me the particulars about when, what time, and any other item that will help us determine just where she was and where she went after she got off work at the Flagship Restaurant?"

"First, are you sure that it was Jennifer?"

"I positively know it was Jennifer, because I know her well. She is a bartender at the Flagship and we always speak to each other when we meet here at the station or at the bar at the Flagship."

"Did you ever date her Donald?"

"Oh no, she was older than I am. We were just friends."

"What time do you think it was when she stopped at the station for gas?"

"I'm not positive of the exact time, but I do know that I was preparing to close the station at one thirty, our usual closing time, and she stopped during the time I had started to close up. Jennifer did that periodically. She was very often my last customer and often stopped to get milk and cereal and stuff like that."

"Did you see her get out of the car at the pump?"

"Yes I did. She filled her tank using a credit card and that slip would have the exact time and date, if you need it. I always looked out the window to see who it was, because at that time of the morning, our front door requires me to unlock it by a remote button."

"She came into the store for something, I can't remember exactly what. She usually bought a lottery ticket and cigarettes. Maybe she got a pack of cigarettes or something. I recognized her and opened the door. Mr. Janosik instructed us to always do that."

"Are you sure she was alone, or could there have been someone with her?"

"I could see her well and I saw no one in her car. I also saw her get in the car and drive off but she did get a call on a cell phone when she came in the store; but when she left our lot, she turned around and headed west back toward Seaford. She normally drove south towards Blades. I think she told me that she lives with a roommate in Blades."

"Did you hear any of her conversation on that phone?"

"No, I didn't hear any of the conversation she held on the phone except I did hear her say at the end of her talk, that she would meet whoever it was at the Nanticoke Hospital parking lot and that is west of here. I read that is where they found her car."

"I remember asking her if she had a relative or a friend in the hospital or someone hurt or sick in the hospital, some question like that; anyway, she said no, it was just a friend that she wanted to see and she was going to meet him in the parking lot."

"Did she mention any names? Did she actually say the word him?"

"No, she didn't mention any names but she did say the word him—I am sure of that. I did not ask her who. It was none of my business anyway."

"Thank you Donald you have been very helpful."

After leaving the station, Jack drove to the Nanticoke Hospital just to refresh his memory on the layout of the hospital parking areas. There were several exits from the lot and no guards. Overhead lighting was in the area.

He was considering whether Jennifer could have met someone she knew there and wondered if she could have been raped at the parking lot. He made up his mind that she may just have been raped there and taken to the site where the body was found, in the rapist's own vehicle. If it was dark, she just may have been raped in that lot. He was sure of it because her car was still there.

Yes, he thought, if the station clerk was truthful in what he said, he now had an answer as to how the murderer made contact with her. The person she was to meet at the hospital parking lot may or may not have been the murderer.

At least they now had an answer as how the murderer got to her. There was now an opportunity for someone to get in her car or at least out of her car. He added in his report that it may have been the caller who got her out of her car or someone that got in her car while she was meeting someone there.

There were no fingerprints found on the car. So he added that it appears that the killer had wiped the car clean. There was not even a trace of Jennifer's prints on the steering wheel. He gave a full report to the team and to agent Spedden.

Bob asked Jack, "Was Jennifer's cell phone in the car or in her purse when they found her car? I think that we can get the number that called her when she was in the store."

"Yes, that's a possibility—we have a list of all the contents. Let me check it out."

In a few minutes he returned and stated that there was no money in her purse, but her paycheck was still in her purse as well as her credit cards. Her cell phone was not in her purse or found in any side compartment. The items that were found were also without fingerprints except on a few maps, a lottery ticket, and on a new pack of cigarettes found on the floor.

They were looking for someone who was very careful and evidently knew how to hide evidence except he always left a length of that cable as if he was trying to establish a trademark of his killings as agent Carle had mentioned in the meeting."

CHAPTER TWELVE

AFTER HEARING DETECTIVE TRUITT'S REPORT, Bob Spedden arranged a meeting with Jennifer's parents in Laurel, Delaware. He also instructed agent Milligan to retrieve all the files that were available on the rape and murders of Harriet O'Brien and Jeanne Records that were killed last year.

The fact that they were both strangled by the same type wire cable that was used by the killer on the new girl, Jennifer indicated that all may have been killed by the same person.

"Bob, I think we can absolutely state now, that those two girls were killed by the same person that killed Jennifer. That certainly proves, in my opinion, that Horace could not have been the killer of those two women. I am also positive that we have a serial rapist and killer on the loose around here. Let's not publish this information just yet."

"Mr. and Mrs. Collins, I am Robert Spedden of the FBI and first I want you to know that I am very sorry in having to talk to you about your daughter Jennifer, but we are determined to find the person responsible for her death soon. Does it suit you to talk to me for a few minutes so we can determine if you have any information that may help us in finding the individual?"

Mr. Collins answered, "Yes, now is okay, my wife and I are very anxious to learn who could have done this. Jennifer didn't have an enemy in the world. She was a very nice girl and everyone liked her. She was to be married to Richard Bennett, who is in Alaska right now working for an oil company."

"He was to return to Bridgeville, in about two weeks. My wife talked with him on the phone the day after the police found her body. Richard is very distressed about her death, and promised us that he would come see us on the 23rd when he returns for a few weeks of vacation time. They were to have been married at that time."

"So you did call him and tell him about Jennifer's death and you did say he was in Alaska working when she was killed?"

"Yes, Mr. Spedden that is right, I called him."

"Do you have any idea or thoughts as to who could have done this? We have been told that she was once engaged to someone else? Is that true and if so; what can you tell me about him?"

"Yes that is true, that was over a year ago. She was engaged to a Laurel boy named Fred Messick. He seemed like a nice boy but he could not make a living in Laurel or in the area and decided to move away to a place where he could find work. He was a house painter. Jennifer liked her job at the Flagship Restaurant, and would not go with him. She may have done so later; but she would not leave until he had a job lined up."

"We both thought that was a smart decision at the time. She told him that she would not consider moving until he had a steady job. He was upset and asked her for the engagement ring back. She gave the ring back to him and we have never heard from him since."

"No, Clarence, that is not right. She told me on the telephone that he came in the Flagship one night last week and she saw him there. He said that he wanted to see her again and she told him that she was to be married in a few weeks. She said that he left the restaurant upset. She talked to him the next day on the telephone and she told him that she was going to get. He told her that he had not married anyone and that he wished her well. She said he did not appear to be very upset about her getting married. He also told her that he was working in South Carolina and leaving to go there the next day. He told her that he just wanted to see her once more before he left for Florida. He suggested that he meet her at work but she told him he was wasting his time and he hung up on her. She was hoping that he would not come in the restaurant and make a scene."

"Do you know where he moved to or the date when he left the first time?"

"That was about five or six years ago. I think it was in the summer of 1989, yes it was 1989 because Jenny got that job shortly after she was 21 years old. She became 21 in 1989. She was a waitress before that."

"Jennifer said that someone told her that he went to Florida. But I'm not sure about that. If she knew she never told us. It wasn't long before she met Richard and just last month they agreed to marry."

"You say that she had not heard from him since that time. Do you know if he ever tried to contact Jennifer after he left the first time or after she met him in the bar last week?"

"Not that I am aware of. He probably would have called here if he tried because Jennifer was living with us when he left. He would not have known her new address."

"Does she have a cell phone? He may have tried to call her on that."

"Yes, I guess that is right, he could have done that; but if he did, Jenny never told us about it."

"Mrs. Collins, do you know if Jennifer knew Harriet O'Brien or Jeanne Records? If you will recall, we had two girls and a man murdered in Seaford that were all members of the Class of 1984? I know that your daughter graduated from Laurel, High School; but I am really interested in knowing if your Jennifer knew either of those two girls?"

"Yes, she did Mr. Spedden. Jennifer knew them when they were in high school. My daughter played basketball and so did both of those girls and they played against each other in high school games several times. They of course were on opposite teams because they were on the Seaford team and Jenny was on the Laurel team."

"She told me several times that she had seen them at the restaurant where she worked."

"When did she tell you that?"

"It was some days after it was in the paper that those girls had been raped and murdered. That was about a year ago, I think."

"Back then the newspapers was full of those rapes and murders, I asked Jenny if she knew them, and she said that she did and she told me about their playing basketball when in school. She said that she was still in contact with both of them, because they both came to the place where Jenny worked and they often talked about their schools days."

"Did she mention to you anything about why she thought they may have been murdered?"

"Not that I can think of, but she did tell me that both of them were still single and were still almost inseparable even after several years after they graduated. She also told me that she wondered if they weren't—oh, I shouldn't tell you this."

"What's that Mrs. Collins" You might be surprised how often something that a person thinks is immaterial proves to be just a link to something that helps us find what we are looking for."

"Well, she told me that she wondered if they were lesbians. She was confused about that because they were both dating men but she said that some lesbians do in fact date men some times."

"Yes, we have been told that they were very close friends by almost everyone we interviewed, but from our investigation we pretty much eliminated that possibility."

"Speaking of interviews we conducted at that time, we interviewed all the employees of the Flagship Restaurant. Do you know if we interviewed Jennifer about those murders last year?"

"Yes, you did, she was excited about that because all the employees were wondering if one of their fellow workers was the guilty one. They were afraid to be alone when they left work. Oh, dear Mr. Spedden could one of them have killed our Jenny?"

"We don't know that, but we are looking into all possibilities. That is why we are talking to you. We just hope that these interviews will eventually give us answers to our questions and lead us to the guilty person. I will pull the files of last year and read what Jennifer told us at that time."

"Thank you Mr. and Mrs. Collins. I want you to know that we will find this man and bring him to justice. If you hear or think of anything else that may help us in our search, please take this card and call me at any time. It is my cell phone number. Chief Daley of the Seaford Police Department told me that Jennifer's personal items would be released to you in a few weeks."

"Does that include her automobile?"

"Yes."

"Great, it wasn't paid for yet so I did call the bank, and I paid her last payment. I will sell it."

"Thanks again and I want you to know that I am confident that we will have the killer of your daughter in jail soon."

Bob returned to the police station to transcribe his interview with Mr. and Mrs. Collins and he found the interview that was conducted by Jack Truitt of the Seaford police last year. That interview mentioned nothing new at the time; but there was a note made by Detective Truitt that Jennifer appeared to be very upset when she was being interviewed and when he asked Jennifer if there was something wrong she told him, that she was upset because she and her boyfriend had just broken up. Her boyfriend's name was Fred Messick."

"Fred Messick again could not be found to be interviewed. A friend of Fred's, Ted Larson of Laurel, reported when interviewed that Fred was in Atlantic City gambling the week of the Class Reunion murders and he had just left to move to Florida to find work the day before he was interviewed. Fred's presence in Atlantic City was confirmed at the time by entries on his credit card provided by the bank. There was no further reference to Fred Messick in the report."

Bob made a note in his new report that if this friend's story and the alibi confirmation on his being in Atlantic

City were correct then Fred could not have been involved in the deaths of the two women. That alibi needed to be looked at again. There had to be an error with that alibi. He asked agent Milligan to check that out again.

Bob turned his attention back to the man who reported seeing Jennifer at the service station the night she was first reported missing.

Donald Jenkins was probably the last person to have seen Jennifer alive so they would have to do a background check on Mr. Jenkins. He added in the report that he doubted Mr. Jenkins was involved because he had volunteered a lot of information that put him into the picture. If he was involved he surely would not have mentioned what he did; but he was to be added to the list of suspects along with this painter Fred Messick anyway. Fred being in Atlantic City had them all confused. Could they be wrong in suspecting him of this new murder?

Agent Spedden was discussing the details with the team when a call was received from the Police chief in the neighboring town of Laurel. He said that a girl's body had just been found in the State Park at Trap Pond, east of Laurel, and that she had been raped and murdered in a similar method, by strangulation, as was the Seaford lady. He was wondering if there was a connection to the murder in Seaford.

Bob immediately left for Laurel to study the situation.

Chief Henry Hickman of the Laurel Police Department advised Bob that the victim, Rosalie Ellis was 24 years old and married with one child, which was two years old. Her husband Dallas Ellis told the Laurel police that Rosalie had left the house shortly after 10:30 pm in the family car. She was going to pick up a few items from a local corner grocery after he got home from a meeting at their church.

She did not return home from the store and after several hours he found her car parked in the store's parking lot and he reported her missing to the city police.

Her purse was found on the ground under her car. There was no money in her purse. It appeared that she was attacked at her car as she was getting out of her car and robbed. She was evidently taken to Trap Pond in another vehicle.

The store manager said that he had not seen anything out of the ordinary in the lot. He stated that there was always a lot of activity in his parking area adding that it appeared to be a meeting place for many people every night; especially the youth and the migrant workers.

He said that he had reported to the Seaford police on several occasions that the migrant workers were using his lot for parking and a place to be drinking. He suspected some drug activity also. It was hurting his business.

Later when he was shown the picture of Rosalie, he said he remembered seeing the girl in the store many times but he could not help them determine if she had come in the store the night before she was listed as missing.

The wire used to strangle Rosalie appeared to be identical to the wire found on the female victims in the

Seaford Class reunion murders of the year before and the same as used in the strangulation of Jennifer two weeks earlier.

It was now very apparent a serial murderer was active in the area and the newspapers all had front page headlines the next morning that read 'Serial Killer' Strikes Again.

Special Agent, William Carle, the Wilmington Branch FBI chief, detailed two additional agents to work the Seaford and Laurel murders and a report of the method of killing and the actual wire used, was sent to the Washington DC FBI headquarters for comparison to others held in evidence.

A request for information was also made to determine if any other murder cases were still open, especially on the East Coast where a similar wire was found in the various reports.

Agent Carle then went to Seaford to talk to Bob Spedden and to take the additional agents to Seaford. He scheduled a meeting with Laurel's Police Chief Henry Hickman.

"Chief we are working on your case as a possible killing by a serial killer. As you probably know, there is an open case in Seaford, where three women were apparently killed by the same person who killed your Laurel woman."

"Yes, I am aware of that possibility and I have been in contact with Chief Daley in Seaford. He told me that the two girls killed in Seaford last year also were being reopened because their deaths were apparently by the same person."

"Yes that is true, but we still have several unanswered questions that need to be answered before we can officially make that announcement. One of the questions we have on last year's case is how one of the Seaford girl's automobile got to Laurel. If you will recall it was found in the Centenary Church parking lot."

"Yes, I remember that and our police department wondered at that time if it got there by someone from Laurel. Perhaps our question at that time was right. He may be the same guy that raped and killed our young lady."

"Yes Chief, we too have given thought to that; but our problem is that the Laurel man we thought may have committed the murder of our recent lady, Jennifer Collins, was reported as being in Atlantic City, New Jersey the nights when the two women were raped and murdered. I might add that he was a Laurel man at that time. I will see that you get a copy of that transcript."

"I have assigned three of my agents to these cases and agent Robert Spedden is heading up our FBI investigations in both cases. Because of the possibility that we may have a serial killer in the area, he will be assisting your office and all of our services will be at your disposal."

The secretary in the police station knocked on the door and told chief Hickman that Mr. Carle had a long distance call.

"Thank you Mary, transfer the call to my private line in my office. Mr. Carle you can take the call in my office. Use the white phone."

"Thank you chief."

Bill took the call from the FBI headquarters in Washington DC and was told that they were faxing to the Seaford Police Chief six open murder cases that may possibly be connected to the Seaford case because they were all unsolved cases and a similar wire cable was used to kill all of the six women. All of the women had been raped.

Bill told then to send a duplicate of the fax to Chief Hickman in Laurel and agent Nelson Parham who had just been reassigned to work with the Laurel investigations.

Chief Hickman said that he would have an office prepared for agent Parham. Agents Gary Titus and Claude Nickerson would be based in the Seaford Command Center, but would work with him and agent Parham in Laurel as well. All agents would copy progress reports to the Wilmington branch through Bob Spedden or Nelson Parham.

In a matter of minutes the faxes were received and the six possible unsolved murders were all young women ages 21 to 27. Three of the murders were in Florida. One of those three was in Gainesville, and two in Tampa. Another was in Macon, Georgia, and the other two were in North Carolina at Raleigh.

The transcripts were reviewed and five of the murders had enough similarities to warrant additional investigation as possibly being connected to the lower Delaware murders.

The unsolved murder in Macon, Georgia was set aside for the present time because it was not a rape case and the strangulation was by a belt not by a wire.

The two murders in Raleigh were of women that were known dealers in drugs and they were killed in a purchase of drugs that went sour. There was no rape involved in either case but both were strangled to death by a wire. The wire was not a perfect match.

Bob told agent Carle, "I am going to contact the local authorities on all six of the cases starting with the ones in Florida. If you will remember, one of our suspects in the Seaford Class Reunion case lived in Tampa, Florida. He was the drug addict who was a member of the high school class who was arrested in Delaware for trafficking drugs."

Bob suggested, "Perhaps we should check up on those two deaths in Raleigh anyway. They just may be connected to the drug addict, Harry Black, in our Seaford cases."

"Yes, I will contact headquarters about that."

"There just may be a connection between the murders in Tampa and the ones in Delaware. I really don't think that he is the murderer but he may have some information on them. His name was Harry Black, remember him?"

"Yes I remember Harry, he's the gay guy and I feel sure that he is not our man; but that's a good place to start. He may know someone who lives in Tampa or lower Delaware who has lived or visited both places just as he does."

"You know Bob, I just can't get that Seaford man, Oliver Hill out of my mind he was the one with a bad eye. He also drives a pickup truck."

"Yes, I remember Oliver well, but I don't want to get too involved, at the moment, with the same suspects we had in that case."

"However, we should determine if Oliver has been out of Delaware; but first I want to determine if the wire cable used in these two Florida cases is an exact match with that used on the Delaware girls."

"Our lab did confirm that the cable used on the most recent murders in Delaware were a match. If the cable used there in Florida is also a match; then we will have something to go on. That would prove that he was in both Delaware and Florida and we would then need some dates."

"If that turns out to be true, then we do need to get to work on Oliver's whereabouts."

Within a week, the cables used in the Florida murders were examined by the FBI labs and it was found that the wire cable was identical to that used in Delaware. The wire being used had a rubber like cover on it that gave the murderer a good grip on the wire.

They suggested that is why he used the wire.

The cable was very flexible and could be carried in one's pocket with ease. Each piece was about 32 inches long and a match was made on two of the pieces on the end of the cable and it was determined that they were cut from a length of the same cable at some time. It was confirmed that the pieces were cut from the same roll.

It was also determined that the unique cable was manufactured for use on special conveyor systems used in automatic feeders on poultry farms and cattle feeders. Its' manufacturer was in Mobile, Alabama.

"Now we have something to go on. We now know for an absolute fact we have a serial murderer and we need to start connecting these murders. I am confident that our suspect Fred Messick is our rapist and murderer. We have to disprove that Atlantic City question."

"Agent Milligan has compiled a time chart of all the murders that we are aware of and it lists in chronological order all of the murders that we at present are investigating."

"It is now displayed at the Seaford Police Station in the chief's office, and a copy has been placed in the Laurel chief's office as well."

"Our branch offices in those distant offices have been notified and they have all been requested to send copies of all their interviews etc. to Bob Spedden who will head up the complete investigations at all the offices. Bob is heading to Tampa in the morning."

The estimated or confirmed dates on the chart were listed as follows:

Harriet O'Brien, Seaford, Delaware June 19, 1989

Jeanne Records, Seaford, Delaware June 22, 1989
Helen Reeves, St. Petersburg, FL August 23 1989
Mary Hendricks, Tampa, Florida October 25, 1989
Betty Hopkins, Gainesville, FL December 27, 1989
Jennifer Collins, Seaford, Delaware January 3, 1990
Rosalie Ellis, Laurel, Delaware January 6, 1990

"The chart does create a path from mid 1989 to early 1990 and the dates fall into a pattern where the killer was in Delaware in 1989 at the time of our first murders."

"He then was in Florida when winter approached but he returned to Delaware in the middle of the winter in January and that has us puzzled. Why does he travel between those two states?"

"Bob, if Jennifer's old boyfriend is involved maybe he read or learned of her planned marriage to the boy in Alaska, and perhaps that was why he returned to Delaware in the winter."

"Yes, that is definitely a possibility. Please put that in the transcript of the Collins case so we don't lose that thought."

"Gainesville is northeast of Tampa and St. Petersburg, maybe he was on his way back to Delaware. Perhaps Jack is correct about his thought that it was to get Jennifer Collins. We need to follow up on that possibility. That is definitely a possibility we need to check on further right away. Is he still in Delaware or is he on his way south again? If Bill's MO study is correct he may soon be in a 'cooling off' period.

"Bob, it also looks to me like he leaves an area after a few murders to get away from the investigators. The first two that we know of, the Seaford murders, are the only two that were committed within a month or so of each other. If he follows that pattern, I would bet that he is no longer in our area, possibly heading south to Florida as we talk."

"Something that I notice that appears to be repetitive, is that the bodies of all the murders after the first two, Harriet and Jeanne, have apparently been staged in very explicit sexual positions after they were raped and killed. They were probably staged so he could take photos of the victims, or simply to identify the victims as being his. I think he wants us to know which ones he is responsible for."

"I know that sounds silly; but we had a serial killer a few years ago in Florida, who was raping and killing girls at college towns and he too staged his victims, just as our killer is apparently doing. A possible 'copy cat' fixation."

"From what I have read on serial killers, they all have their own way of marking their victims, as if they want everyone to know he was the killer. It's like a game with them."

"Yes, remember that Bill Carle mentioned something about staging in his talk to the team. What we need to do now, is have agent Milligan insert in the chart anything, and I mean anything, that we have a date for in our interviews as well as all events from now onward., Often something will come to light when it is placed in its' proper place."

CHAPTER THIRTEEN

AGENT MILLIGAN INSERTED THE DATES that had been mentioned in all the interviews that had been conducted since the murder of Harriet O'Brien and the clue listing now was displayed in the chief's office.

A meeting of both the Laurel and Seaford police and all the FBI agents was scheduled in the Seaford Police station's conference room. Agent Milligan was awaiting details on several of the reports on the list

1-Harriet O'Brien, Seaford, Delaware June 19, 1989—no staging

2-Jeanne Records, Seaford, Delaware June 22, 1989—no staging

Both were graduates of Seaford High School, 1984
Both were unmarried. Very well liked—Athletic types—
Both found East of Seaford along bank of Nanticoke River—Strangled with same type wire.—Harriet is believed not to have been raped—Jeanne was definitely raped. DNA test results on file. Both thought to have been killed by Horace Hastings, Horace killed by a different person—now in jail. Horace no longer thought to be the killer.

3-Helen Reeves, St. Petersburg, FL August 23, 1989. Body was staged.

Found naked in wooded area.—No evidence of a rape—Autopsy found extremely high alcohol level—Strangled by a wire—DNA found on abdomen of victim was determined to be semen—Body was staged in an explicit sexual sitting position. See photo file Cabinet 12 H Reeves

4-Mary Hendricks, Tampa, Florida October 25, 1989—get files from Tampa

5-Betty Hopkins, Gainesville, FL December 27, 1989—get files from Tampa

6-Jennifer Collins, Laurel, Delaware January 3, 1990—victim staged

Jennifer was last reported seen at a service station/grocery store in Seaford early Friday morning. It was after 1:00 am on the second of January. She received a call on her cell phone. She was to meet the caller at the hospital parking lot.
Jennifer and her new boyfriend were to be married in February 1990. He was in Alaska at the time of her murder.
Jennifer was previously engaged to Fred Messick, a house painter.
Jennifer last seen at a service station/grocery in Laurel after 1:00a.m. January 2
Jennifer and Fred Messick broke their engagement in June 1989 because he wanted her to move south so he could get more work. She refused.

7-Rosalie Ellis, Laurel, Delaware January 6, 1990. She was a married woman whose car was found in a small grocery store parking lot. Body was staged.

The meeting of the two teams was held Monday morning in Seaford and Bob told the members that he would be having a meeting such as this every Monday and on short notice when something was found that all members needed to be informed.

"I find the use of clue listings such as this one very helpful and just now as we were getting the list assembled I think I have a clue that certainly needs to be followed up on right away. Do any of you see what I see in the small chart we already have?"

Agent Milligan, replied, "Well I'm not sure it's the same one you see, but as I was writing it on the chart, I am still concerned about Jennifer's previous boyfriend, Fred Messick, perhaps he was not happy with her not going South with him."

"Detective Truitt said, "Yes I have had him in my mind every since we were told that they broke up."

"Yes, you both are seeing what I see. Now check the dates—Jennifer and Fred broke their engagement in June of 1989, just before we had our first two rapes and murders, so he was in the area at that time. Maybe he wanted to get away from our investigation on the two homicides. Maybe that is why Fred Messick wanted to go to Florida—to get away from his crimes."

"Yes, that is my conclusion also and is one that was not considered in our previous case."

"Gentlemen, I think we have hit a homerun. I see on the list something of extreme value to us. Look at his profession. He was a house painter."

"Just last week we were talking with Steve Cockran about Horace's old pickup truck. He was asking his boss for permission to dispose of it. During that conversation he mentioned that it was last used by a painter that was painting Horace's broiler house roofs."

"Now we know that painter had access to Horace's truck and access to the roll of wire cable that was in the truck and is now missing."

"Thanks to this listing let's expand the list with everything we have and let's get Fred Messick in custody. He is surely the painter who had access to the pickup and is our killer. I am confident that he could not have been in Atlantic City as was reported and we need to prove that. Let's do that immediately."

A wanted notice was issued for Fred Messick, also known as Fred Cassidy.

The former roommate of Fred Messick, George Hearn, in Laurel, Delaware told the investigators that Fred had left Laurel a week ago and that he was not aware where he was going. He stated that he had not seen Fred for over a year when he broke up with his girl friend and when he went south to get a job until he met him in a bar in Seaford and had a beer with him a week or so ago.

When asked if he knew where Fred had moved to when he left Laurel the first time he said that it was in the summer, around June or July and that it was just after he and his girlfriend had broken their engagement. She refused to go to Florida with him until he got a job down there and only after they were married. He thought that it was Tampa, but he wasn't sure about that.

When asked when Fred last came back to Laurel, he said that it was about a week or so ago. He met Fred in a bar in the Hotel Rigbie in Laurel and Fred told him that he was on his way back to South Carolina after visiting his relatives in West Virginia. He was leaving early the next morning.

"Did he have an automobile when you last saw him?"

"No, he was in a pickup truck."

"Can you give us a description of his vehicle?"

"Yes, like I said, it was a pickup truck, a red 1988 Chevrolet half ton. Its cargo area was covered with a white top with windows on the side and at the back. He kept paint supplies in there. He always did keep his pickups very clean and it looked like it was new all the time. He had South Carolina tags on it."

"Did you get real close to the truck and close enough to see the contents in the cargo area?"

"Oh yes, I went out with him after we had a beer and he was telling me that he was still painting and that he had a new pickup. I walked with him to where the truck was parked and we sat in it for a few minutes talking. He had a lot of stuff in there. He always did have a lot of junk in the back of his truck when I worked with him in the past. He told me that he kept a change of clothes in there because he was always messing up the clothes he painted in. I had a feeling that he lived in that truck some times because he even had food in it."

"Tell us about any specific items that you saw in the truck. Did he have any rope or weapons in the truck?"

"I never saw any weapons; but I did see a roll of TV cable and I asked him what he used that cable for. I thought it was a TV cable or something like that. I was wondering if he was working on TV installations or something. He said that he found it at a trash container one time and picked it up because he may find a need for it."

"Can you describe the cable?"

"As best as I can remember; it was rolled up in a cardboard box. It had a black vinyl color covering over the wire—just like I said a TV cable of some type. I don't know anything more than that. In fact that is only what I thought it was."

"Do you recall any other items in there?"

"Well let me think, there was a suitcase, several boxes of food mostly canned, a tool box, lots of paint cans, brushes, and oh yes, he had several cases of beer. That's about all I can think of, oh yes, there was a short handled shovel."

"Thank you, Mr. Hearn. I am leaving my cell phone number on this card and we would appreciate your calling us if you think of anything else about Mr. Messick. Especially call us, if you hear from him or learn of his location."

"Can you tell me why you are looking for him?"

"Yes, Mr. Messick is wanted by us for information that we feel he may have on a case we are working on. We can't say anymore than that."

"I bet he's involved with that girl murdered out at Trap pond last week. All he talked about was sex and how many women he had sex with."

"Did he ever mention any names of any girls?"

"No, he never mentioned names, but he was always talking about them. He was always bragging that he had sex with so many different girls."

"Well Mr. Hearn, we thank you again for the information that you have given us. Should you learn where he is; or anything you think may be of interest to us, do call."

CHAPTER FOURTEEN

A WANTED NOTICE WAS ISSUED FOR Fred Messick as well as a description of his pickup truck. They did not have a photo of Fred and Jennifer's parents said that they did not have a photo of him either but they did give a good description of him.

This description was matched with a description of him given by a second interview with his former roommate George Hearn. Agent Spedden asked detective Truitt if he thought that he could get a picture of Fred from a copy of the Laurel High School Yearbook.

He said he was sure he could find one and Bob said, "We can send that to headquarters and have them age the picture by five or six years."

A request for information by the FBI from the Motor Vehicle Department of the state of South Carolina using what information they had, provided a photo, and his address at the time he licensed his truck was forwarded to Bob Spedden in Seaford.

There was no lien on the title. He bought the truck used from an auto dealer in Columbia who was unable to provide any additional information. This photo and the updated photo from the yearbook were given to the agents for help in identifying Fred.

It was first taken to the Flagship where those who had mentioned Fred as well as Jennifer's parents. All identified the photo as being Fred or the man in the argument on at the Flagship bar.

Wanted posters were now issued with the picture from the South Carolina driver's license and distributed to all authorities up and down the East Coast. Fred Messick was now a wanted man with a price on his capture.

After a meeting with the press, the area newspaper headlines carried the complete story that Fred Messick, a Laurel youth was wanted for a number of rapes and murders from Delaware to Florida and that the FBI had him on their most wanted list as a Serial Rapist and Killer.

The article included a sub title that Horace Hastings was not the killer of Harriet O'Brien and Jeanne Records the previous year and that those two murders were committed by this same Fred Messick.

The story mentioned that the one thing that was not cleared completely was why Horace had called for his employee to drive to Laurel in the early hours to take him home to Seaford, and the fact that Harriet's car was found in Laurel.

The newspapers also wrote about the fact that Fred was previously reported to be in Atlantic City, NJ gambling the week that Jennifer was killed, and that it was found that he had receipts for his stay there during that week. The newspaper was blaming the police for shoddy work in accepting that alibi.

The next day the Police received a visitor from Laurel, Mr. George Hearn, who asked to speak to one of the FBI agents involved with the recent murders. He was sent to the office of Jack Truitt, the town's detective

"Mr. Truitt, I don't know if you remember me, but I was the roommate of Fred Messick for a short time and I was just interviewed a few days ago by one of the FBI men who were asking me about Fred Messick. I read in the paper this morning that Fred was found to have murdered all three of those women and that there was blame being put on your policemen for as they wrote, 'shoddy police work' in proving his alibi."

"Well I got to thinking about that and I tried to remember what I told the FBI about Atlantic City, when they asked me about that a year or so ago."

"From what I read about it, I don't think that what they said about Fred going to Atlantic City is true. His friend Ted Larson was confused. I was the one that went to Atlantic City, not Fred as Ted said."

"What happened was that Fred and I had both planned on going there and Fred used his credit card to guarantee the room. It turned out that Fred and his girl broke up that week, and he was so upset about that he decided to leave for the South to get a job and get away from Seaford. He left Laurel a day or two later, not for Atlantic City, but to go south."

"He told me to take the room—which I did. I would have told you about this sooner if I knew that you were actually looking for Fred."

Detective Truitt called in agent Spedden and had Mr. Hearn repeat what he had just told him.

"Mr. Hearn it was I that interviewed you last year and I will check the transcript of that interview to see where we were on the wrong track. We certainly thank you for coming in and telling us, not because we were catching some heat over that error, but because it puts to rest a problem we had. We are going to have to see that such errors do not happen again. I should have got into that the other day when we talked."

A copy of the truck registration was faxed and the South Carolina tag number was identified and immediately sent to the police departments in all the states between Delaware and Florida along with a wanted notice with the photo from the South Carolina driver's license.

The address listed on the title was at a boarding house in Columbia and there was no trace there to Fred Messick. The owner of the boarding house said that he remembered Fred as being there and he thought Fred was in Columbia working on a paining job at the time. He added that he had allowed him to paint the exterior wood work on his building in exchange for a month's rent.

He had no idea of who else he was working for during his stay there. He checked his records and said that he was a boarder in the house during the period of June 28 through August 24 of 1989. He did not leave a forwarding address.

Bob had the FBI agent in South Carolina make an inquiry of the Columbia Police department as well as the state Police, to determine if Fred had been involved in any problems during his stay in South Carolina, and no record was found.

When asked if there had been any murders or rapes in the Columbia area during that period. The FBI was told that there was one murder but that case was now closed and the suspect was a drug dealer and he admitted the murder. He was now in prison. There was also an attempted rape of a nineteen year old girl that escaped from her attacker and the rapist was unknown. That case was unsolved.

Bob asked the FBI agent in South Carolina to interview the girl in that case to determine if there was a possibility that she may have been attacked by Fred Messick. The girl was a college student named Julia Perry and arrangements were made with her for an interview.

Before leaving for the interview with Miss Perry, Bob was told that he was wanted on the telephone. It was the Seaford Police Department calling.

"Bob, this is Chief Daley in Seaford, I have some very good news for you."

"Don't tell me you have Fred in custody!"

"No, I do wish I could tell you that but I thought I would call so you could rest well tonight after I tell you that you can forget about the mystery we had on Horace and Harriet's red convertible."

"We now know what happened and we no longer have to fear trying to explain that to a smart ass lawyer in a trial."

"Oh wonderful, I can't tell you how many times I really have lost sleep knowing that I may have to explain that to a jury or a lawyer. What happened?"

"Well a boating friend of Horace's had picked up Horace that morning to do some fishing in the ocean. They were having a good day and stayed much longer then they had planned. When they dropped off a buddy in Georgetown, they went on to Laurel and Horace told his friend that because it was so late he could just drop him off in Laurel and go on home to Salisbury instead of having to take him to Seaford only to drive back thru Laurel. He told him that he would call his farm employee to come pick him up."

"Well that would explain it; but why did Horace tell his employee that his truck had broken down?"

"I asked him that very question and he said that he would hate for Horace to call his employee to do that and Horace told his friend Oh, don't worry about that, I'll make up some kind of story to get him to come down. He will do it, he knows who pays him."

"He said that after Horace made the call he went on to Salisbury and left Horace on the Hotel Rigbie porch."

Bob made a call to tell Bill Carle the news on his way to do his interview. Bill was excited and called his home to tell Helen.

"Miss Perry, I am Bob Spedden and this is George Stevens, we are agents of the Federal Bureau of Investigation out of our Columbia office, and we are investigating a series of rapes and murders up and down the Eastern States and we are wondering if your case could possibly be connected to those cases."

"Well Mr. Stevens I wasn't raped my attacker was not successful in raping me."

"Yes, I am aware of that, I have a copy of the report that you gave to the Columbia police after the incident, but I am anxious to hear the details from you because you may just mention something that will help us in our investigation."

"If your attacker was the same man that we are investigating you are one lucky lady, because he has raped a number of women and all of them were killed."

"With that said, would you in your own words, tell me about what happened that night? I think it was July 6th of last year. Is that correct?"

"Yes, it was on July 6, of last year and I was getting in my car after shopping at the Walmart store off 88th Street. When I bent over to load my purchases on the back seat of my car, He grabbed me from behind and put his hand over my mouth so I couldn't yell for help. He opened the door on his pickup truck and pulled me in on the seat."

"Did he drag you to his pickup? You said that he pulled you in on the seat. Was that the seat of your car or the pickup?"

"It all happened so fast I find it hard to remember exactly how it happened; but he was parked just one space away from where I was parked and he didn't have far to pull me. He got in the pickup and pulled me in after him. That much I do remember. I had bruises on my left thigh after it was all over. He reached over me to close the door and then tied my hands with a wire."

"Can you describe the wire he used to tie your hands?"

"It wasn't a rope. I think it was a length of a TV cable or telephone extension wire. I think he must have been a telephone man or a TV repairman. That's what I told the police too."

"Did he have any kind of weapon?"

"Not that I am aware of. He never showed one to me if he did."

"Then what did he do Miss Perry?"

"He pulled me over toward him. I was on my side so I couldn't get up and he drove to the place where he tried to rape me"

"That was on a dirt road off highway 16. Is that correct?"

"Yes, it was a wooded area and I was able to hide from him in the woods when I got away from him."

"How did you do that Miss Perry, Get away from him?"

"When he pushed me out of the pickup, I fell on the ground and he turned me over on my back and untied my hands. He told me that if I behaved myself, he would not hurt me and he told me to take off my slacks which I started to do but I saw a rock about the size of a baseball and I grabbed it as he bent over me and I hit him hard on the head with it."

"He fell on top of me but I got out from under him and I noticed that he was out cold but he was still breathing. His head was bleeding badly. I gave him quite a hit. I pulled up my slacks and ran down the dirt road toward the highway. I hid in the woods for quite a long while until I saw him driving out the road very fast. I watched him until he got on the highway and was out of sight."

"I then walked out of anyone's sight from the highway near the woods, until I got to a service station that was closed. Luckily there was an outside public telephone there. I called 911 and the police came to pick me up. I never saw the man again."

"Did you notice what color the truck was and the make?"

"Yes, it was a red Chevrolet with South Carolina tags, but I did not get the number, I was too scared."

"I have here your description of the man. Please look over your statement and tell me if you have anything to add or change."

After reading her statement given to the State Police, she said, "That's as good as I can describe him. I have nothing to add."

Agent Stevens showed Miss Perry the FBI enhanced picture of Fred Messick from the year book with a photo taken from his South Carolina driver's license. She took a look at them both and said, "Oh my God, that's him—who is he?"

"He's Fred Messick from Delaware and Florida and a mass rapist and murderer. Yes, Miss Perry you are one lucky woman."

Back in the Columbia Police Station, Agent Stevens asked the officers, "Did you by chance make a search of the area and find the cable that Miss Perry said was used to tie her hands?"

"Yes, we did search the area for clues but we found no wire as she described. We did find the rock she claimed she hit him with, and there were small spots of blood on it. We have a DNA report from that. We also checked the area hospitals to see if anyone came in for treatment of a head wound. There was none."

The full transcript was faxed to agent Robert Spedden at the Seaford Police Department in Delaware.

CHAPTER FIFTEEN

A GENT SPEDDEN CALLED HIS TEAM together and read the transcripts to them.

"Men, we now are quite sure that Fred Messick is once again our prime suspect and a wanted poster has been issued for his arrest. We have his vehicle tag number and the color of his truck. I am hoping that will locate our man very quickly."

"But we still have one item here in Seaford that requires to be certified. We have a written statement from Fred's roommate, George Hearn that Fred Messick who was reported to have been in Atlantic City during the week that Harriet and Jeanne were killed in Seaford last year was in fact not in Atlantic City as we thought."

"When we checked that report before, Fred had motel charges on his credit card to back up the report that he was indeed there. Mr. Hearn now tells us that he and a friend are the ones who went to Atlantic City and stayed in a room that Fred had already guaranteed on his credit card. I hope this statement is true but we must have it confirmed. We need to confirm that statement so that it cannot be questioned by a jury."

"Mr. Hearn said that he and a friend were there and not Fred. The two of then went to Atlantic City and used the reservation that Fred had guaranteed on his credit card. We need to contact that friend and to determine if they have anything to back up this new claim. Was Fred in Atlantic City when Jennifer was killed?"

"His roommate in Laurel gave us the story I just mentioned that Fred was not in Atlantic City but again we need proof of that statement."

"Everything certainly points to Fred as being our killer, but we must prove that statement of his roommate. A lawyer would certainly tell us to prove it. If that is true, then Fred could have been in Seaford when the girls were killed. Let's check out the roommate's claim that Fred was not in Atlantic City."

"Bob, I have a question about all this too. Last year I examined Fred's credit card statement with the bank, and I found only a single payment for his motel room and there were no other charges in Atlantic City. There were no other charges on his credit cards until June 29th in Delmar, Delaware for gasoline, and another on July 1st for a purchase of gasoline in Emporia Virginia. I think that will prove that he was not in Atlantic City when Jennifer was killed."

"That first purchase was the day that Jennifer is reported as having been killed. That would put him back in Delaware on the date of her death and apparently heading south. This appears to answer your question."

"Well Jack that certainly answers our question about his alibi of being in Atlantic City doesn't it? I wonder just where he is now. I would suspect that he is now in Florida or some other southern location but we still need to verify that his friends were in Atlantic City as they claim."

The credit cards of both the friends later revealed charges in Atlantic City on the dates in question. They had used their cards for dinners at the casino. The agents were now satisfied that Fred was in Delaware at the time the two women were killed.

A meeting of the team was interrupted when the chief's clerk, knocked on the door and told Mr. Spedden that he had a call from the FBI office in Richmond, Virginia.

"Mr. Spedden, This is Agent Richard Selby, of the Richmond office. We have the truck you have posted as being wanted in our custody. It was found parked in Richmond in the parking lot of a local shopping center."

"We placed a team of agents watching the truck for a period of 48 hours. There was no attempt by anyone to enter the truck. We are of the opinion that the truck has been abandoned."

"Were there any contents in the cargo area?"

"Just a lot of old stuff, used paint brushes and a bag of trash that included empty beer cans, a half eaten sandwich, several credit cards that had been cut up beyond recognition, but the remains have been sent to DC for an attempt in putting the parts together."

"Then it appears that the owner is aware that we were looking for him."

"Yes apparently. I would guess that he saw one of the overhead alerts on the interstate that had his truck description and license tag number on it."

"Mr. Selby, the owner of that truck is a prime suspect in a number of rapes and murders. Should you have and rapes or murders in your area, please call this office immediately. I will forward you a brief report on this individual by fax. Can you tell me if there was a partial roll of wire that may look like a TV cable in the truck?"

"There was no such wire or cable in the truck. I think the contents of value were probably removed. Do you have any suggestions as to how we can help you from this end?"

"Yes, I would appreciate a check of nearby motels, truck rentals or sales. The man, Fred Messick, is a painter by profession and in as much as his cargo area was almost empty I would guess that he transferred his equipment to another pickup or panel truck. The FBI will contact you soon about what to do with the truck. In the meantime have it placed under your supervision."

The next day, Agent Selby again called the Seaford office of the Police chief, and asked to speak again to agent Spedden.

"Bob, we placed a news item in the local paper and the TV people picked up on the release. Then just a few minutes ago we got a call from a local man, that he had witnessed a man transferring contents of the truck we now have in custody to another pickup. We have no information as to color, model or maker. So at this point all I can tell you is that your suspect is in another pickup and that pickup was not a new truck."

"Thank you Richard, I will be sending agent George Milligan of my office to meet with you and you may want to pick him up at the airport. His flight number will be faxed to you as soon as we have it all set up. His flight will be out of Baltimore Maryland."

"Great I will have him picked up. We are attempting to obtain information on the new truck, but no luck at this time."

"If our suspect continues his actions of the past, he is probably preparing for another rape and murder so you can see why we are so anxious to find where he is. We expect another attack any day now."

Back in Laurel, Delaware the team was doing an extensive investigation on Fred Messick. It was determined that he was a graduate of the Laurel high school, in 1983, and the week after his graduation he went to Norfolk, Virginia and was hired by National Construction Company as a painter.

He worked for them for three years and was fired for repeated absences from work, and drinking on the job.

Since that time he earned a living doing small painting jobs in Sussex and Wicomico counties in Delaware and

Maryland. He had been arrested two times for driving under the influence, and was once charged with physical abuse of a female, but the girl refused to prefer charges. This was a battery case. There was no attempt to rape her.

His parents were from West Virginia and they had returned there in 1984. Fred did not go with them because he was working for the Construction Company who was building a large Condo complex in Ocean City, Maryland just off the ocean, and he was making good money. He joined the union but rarely attended any union meetings.

After he was fired, he started painting on small jobs locally and then in 1989 he left Laurel owing his roommate his half of the month's rent.

All of the data collected confirmed that Fred was in the areas of the murders and a nationwide alert was issued for his arrest and the search efforts were publicized in the newspapers and on TV. He was given the moniker 'The Class Reunion Rapist" and considerable coverage on him and the known cases was reported in the newspapers and on TV.

Fred himself became aware that he was wanted for rape and murder when he saw the story on the TV station in Richmond, Virginia. He knew he had to quit using his credit cards and decided that he would have to get a different vehicle as they most likely had identified what he was driving.

He had less than two hundred dollars left from his last salary payment. He had to have more money to keep ahead of those tracking him and he knew that he had to quit using his credit card to eliminate his charges to serve as a means of tracking his every move.

He had nothing to lose so he decided to get some money from stores. He had a pistol and decided that he would search for a likely prospect to get the needed cash.

He parked his pickup in a mall parking lot and went into the mall and had a sandwich. He found that a bus stop was available at a stop in front of the mall. He then took a bus down the street eyeing possible prospects to rob. He noticed an auto rental and got off the bus at the next intersection, and made a rental of an automobile for the day. He used that vehicle to return to his prospective money source, liquor stores and groceries, and eventually his old truck.

The newspapers the next morning reported a series of robberies in northeast Richmond and Fred was in an almost new pickup truck with a registration card and Virginia tags issued to Martin Sammons of Richmond, Virginia. He was now a new man with a Virginia driver's license. Fred Messick was now a known felon and he knew that he had to stay ahead of the police in his every move.

He was happy that he had transferred the contents of his pickup to this new truck because when he went back to check on the truck, it was gone. After several weeks of several small robberies around Richmond, he had enough cash to stop running and to have a good time. He drove south down Interstate 95.

CHAPTER SIXTEEN

I T HAD BEEN OVER A month without a trace of Fred Messick. The FBI agents that were working in Seaford and Laurel were recalled to the Wilmington branch office, satisfied that they now knew who their murderer was.

Agents Bob Spedden was sent to Florida to interview those involved with the rapes and murders in Florida. It was thought that Fred was probably living in Florida and they were hoping that he just may make contact with some of his acquaintances there. He reported to the Tampa FBI branch office.

He was assigned to the team of the office that was working on the Florida rapes and murders which had evidence pointed to Fred Messick. The team was headed up by agent Charles O'Neal.

Agents Charles O'Neal and Robert Spedden were interviewing the parents of Mary Hendricks who had been raped and murdered in Tampa, Florida on October 25, 1989.

"Mr. and Mrs. Hendricks, I have with me today, agent Robert Spedden who is an FBI agent out of our Wilmington

Delaware branch office. I know that we have met with you many times and have asked you a lot of questions, but once again, we would like to talk to you about your daughter Mary, who was raped and murdered back in October."

"Mr. Spedden is working on a similar case up in Delaware and on several other similar cases that may, and I repeat may, be connected to the man than killed your daughter Mary. We are attempting to tie together a series of rapes and murders that we now feel may have been committed by the same individual. Would you please hear his questions and assist us in getting these murders resolved?"

"Mr. O'Neal we are very pleased to hear that you all are still working on the killer of our daughter. It has been several months now and we had about given up on finding out who did this terrible thing to our little Mary. We are anxious to help in any way we can."

"Okay, Mrs. Hendricks. Let me begin by telling you that we are indeed on the track of that man. We feel that we know for sure who her murderer was. All we need to do now is to find him and we are hoping that you or some of Mary's friends may be able to give us some information that might lead us to where he is. Once we find where he is, it will be just a matter of time before we have him behind bars."

"Oh how happy we will be to see him get what he deserves. We will have no peace until he is behind bars. Are you able to tell me who it is?"

"I do wish that I could do that but I am sure you can understand why we can't do that before we have him locked up."

"Tell me, can you recall any events near the last time you saw Mary? Who she was with? Where she was supposed to be on that evening? I know that you have probably told Mr. O'Neal the answers to many of the questions I am about to ask you but it is important that I have your answers again, because I am looking for anything that will give me a picture of exactly what happened that night. We may be able to put together some information that will lead us to our killer."

"Her best friends were Kitty Titus, Beatrice Green, and Karen McFarland. The four of them were friends from high school. All are still unmarried and they enjoyed each other's company."

"The night that we last saw Mary, the four of them went to see a movie and I suppose they went to Rachael's Club on Silverside Avenue, at least we were told by the police that they went there. I don't know that for sure. We do know that they frequently went to those dance clubs together."

"Mary called me after she had been to the movies, and she told me that it would be after midnight before she got home as they were going to the Club for dancing. I am not certain which club it was so I assume the police are right in saying Rachael's. I do know they go there often together. The four of them did that often. Needless to say that is the last time I talked with her."

"Did any of the four have regular dates?"

"Yes, I know for sure that Karen did because Mary told me that she was going to get married at Christmas, and she was indeed married to Frank Petrino the week of Christmas. Our daughter Mary was dating a boy name Oscar Fortner but she was not with him that last evening. He is a pilot for Delta Airlines. I don't know if the other girls have steady dates or not."

"When did you report Mary as missing Mrs. Hendricks?"

"I was deeply concerned when she did not get home before 1:00 am as she had told me to expect her on the phone earlier, but I did not call the police until the next morning after I got a call from Kitty Titus asking to talk with Mary. I told her that Mary was not at home yet and I wondered what had happened to her."

"Kitty told me that Mary left the club at midnight and had told her that she had a ride home. She was dancing with a guy a lot during the evening and Kitty said she assumed that was who was to take her home."

"Do you have Kitty's telephone number and address?"

"I don't, but I will check Mary's telephone and address book. I am sure she has them. Wait just a second and I will go get it to see if its' in there."

Mrs. Hendricks returned with the small book and told agent Spedden, "Yes I have both right here. Would you like to copy them down?"

"Yes, thanks Mrs. Hendricks that will be a lot of help to me. I do want to talk with her and the other girls that went to the club with her. They may give us some information which may help us determine who the man was who was supposedly taking her home."

"The other three girl's address and telephone numbers are also in the book if you want them."

"Yes, I was going to ask you about them too."

The agents copied the numbers and addresses from Mary's book and just on a thought at the moment, agent Spedden, turned to the B listings and his hunch was correct. There in Mary's address book, was a telephone number for a Harry Black. There was no address listed. Bob copied that number also without making any comment.

"Mr. and Mrs. Hendricks, I am certain that we will soon have the man who did this terrible thing to your daughter and we want to thank you for talking with us. We know how hard that is to do. Our office will advise you as soon as we have this guy in jail."

The two agents returned to the Tampa office and placed calls to all three of the other girls and arrangements were to meet with each one of them at different times.

The first interview was with Kitty Titus, as she definitely knew about Mary going home with someone else.

"Miss Titus, we understand that you went to Rachel's Club in Tampa with Mary Hendricks the night that she was reported missing. Is that true/"

"Yes, I did and so did two of my friends, Karen McFarland and Bea Green."

"We have a report that Mary left the club with a man who offered to take her home. Can you confirm that statement?"

"Oh yes, that is true. Mary seemed to be attracted to him and spent most of the evening dancing with the man."

"Do you by chance, know the man's name or where he lives?"

"I don't know the man, but I have seen him at the club many times in the past several years. He's a nice looking man, very friendly guy, and everyone calls him Freddie. That is about all I know about him. Oh yes, he does have a rather deep scar over his right eyebrow."

"How big would you estimate that scar to be?"

"I would guess that it is about an inch long."

"Was Mary playing around with drugs? Could Freddie actually be a drug dealer? I have reports that Rachael's has quite a lot of drug users who hang out there."

"Yes, there are a lot of drug users as well as dealers hanging around there just as there are at any such club in the area. But I can tell you for certain that Mary certainly did not do drugs. Nor do the other three of us girls. We go there to dance and have fun with others our age. We love the music."

"We do have a few drinks at times and on occasion we do date someone we meet at the clubs, except Karen, she had a steady guy and she is now married. Her married name is Petrino. She does not go to the club now unless her husband is home and takes her. He is an airline pilot and away a lot."

"On the night that Mary disappeared, did you see Mary leave the club with this Freddie?"

"Yes, I did. The three of us were concerned for Mary, because we felt she had too much to drink and we were concerned that Freddie might try to take advantage of her."

"Did you tell the police about your concerns?"

"I know I didn't. I wasn't asked, and I would not want anyone to know that. She was a very nice girl and never got that way before. I think that Freddie had something to do with her getting too much to drink and probably her death and I did tell the police that."

"Yes, I know, I have the transcript of your interview with detective Willis. The problem we have with all of this Miss Titus is that we don't know where Freddie lives. Can you give us any information about that?"

"No, I don't know where he lives, and I have not seen him at Rachael's since that night; but Bea Green and I were at the Tropic Club about a month or so later and she said that she saw Freddie leaving the club with Harry."

"Harry who Miss Titus?"

"Harry Black, he has the group that plays at many of the clubs here in Tampa and St. Pete. Harry is gay and we were wondering if he and Freddie were leaving for—well you know what I mean."

"Have you seen them together before?"

"No, and I didn't see them leave but Bea said that it definitely was Freddie."

"Thank you Miss Titus, you have been very helpful to us. I now ask that if you see Freddie again, that you call us as soon as possible. We want to talk to him about Mary Hendricks and the night that he took her home."

"Mr. Spedden, he didn't take her home or at least she didn't get there. That was the night she disappeared."

"Yes, we are aware of that, but she did leave the club with him and we want to know where they went. Here's my card with my cell phone number—if you see Freddie anywhere at any time, please call me immediately. Don't tell Freddie we are looking for him."

Later that afternoon, agents O'Neal and Spedden met with Beatrice Green at her apartment in Clearwater, Florida"

"Miss Green, since I last talked to you, shortly after the death of your friend Mary Hendricks, we have received some information that may lead us to her killer and we would like to talk to you to see if you can confirm any of the data that we now have. This is special agent Robert Spedden, also of the FBI and he has some questions. Are you free to talk to us for a few minutes?"

"Absolutely, I sure hope that you find her killer, we girls are scared to death about going out anymore."

"Miss Green, We have a report that perhaps you saw a guy named Freddie recently at the Tropic Club and that he was with a musician named Harry Black. Is that true?"

"Yes I saw him at the Tropic Club just a week ago. I know it was him because I saw the scar on his forehead. He was with Mary the night that she disappeared. I saw them leave. He was driving a pickup truck. I couldn't believe that Mary would go out with a guy in such a dirty pickup truck."

"I started to call the police when I saw Harry and Freddie, but I was afraid to get involved. I did tell the girls though. I guess one of them told you that."

"Yes, that is correct. If you ever see him again, please get in touch with us immediately. We want to talk to him about Mary. As far as we know he was the last person to see her alive."

"You mentioned that he had a very dirty truck. Can you give me a description of the truck he was in?"

"Well it wasn't dirty in the sense of actual dirt or grime, what I meant was that it was full of stuff. It had a cover, one of those white hard tops with windows and a tail gate door and you could see that it was full of everything. I think that he must have been living in it."

"Do you know what kind of truck or color it was?"

"The truck was a faded maroon color and as I said the topper was white. I don't know one truck from another but it did have Utah tags on it. The one with a bee hive on it."

"We were also told that he was with Harry Black, the musician at the various clubs as you just said. What can you tell us about Harry?"

"Well Harry plays in bands at several of the clubs that we frequent. We love to hear him play. But he is known to have been a drug dealer, but we girls don't do drugs and I haven't seen any evidence of him doing that. He is also reported to be gay, and when I saw him leave with Freddie we were wondering if Freddie was also gay and if he was simply messing with Harry. We were laughing about that."

"You said we, who else was with you?"

"Oh sorry, it was Karen McFarland. We stopped in only for a beer. Karen doesn't do the clubs anymore, she's married now."

"Do you know Harry very well or just see him at the clubs?"

"Like I said earlier, I see him at the various clubs that we attend. He is a great musician but they claim that he messes with drug and has some bad friends. They say he is gay. I have never let myself get friendly with such people. That's all, I just see him at the clubs when dancing and I think he recognizes us as being regular customers. I doubt if he even knows any of our names."

"You said he was gay. How do you know that he's gay?"

"To tell you the truth, I don't know, but everyone says he is. That's all I know. He seems to like the men and is always playing up to them when he's not playing in the band. I would bet he is gay."

"Would you say that he and Freddie are friends?"

"I can't say that. I have only seen them together that one time. I see Freddie at the different clubs and Harry is not with him. I have only seen them together that one time and they were leaving the club as we went in."

"You said that you saw Harry and Freddie leave the Tropic Club. Can you try to remember exactly when that was?"

"I'm not sure, but I do know that it was on a Saturday afternoon, because Karen and I had just finished doing some shopping and we were hot and tired. We both work during the week days. We decided to get a beer and rest before going to Countryside Mall in Clearwater where a sale was going on to finish our shopping."

"We stopped at the club on our way to Clearwater. There was no dancing or music because it was in the afternoon. Perhaps Karen can give you the exact date."

"Thank you Miss Green, Your information may help us find Mary's killer. If you remember anything else about seeing Harry or Freddie please give us a call, and if you see Freddie at any of your clubs in the future please slip out and give us a call immediately. It is very important that we talk with him. Please tell no one that we are looking for Freddie or Harry."

The Agents decided to check with agent Charles Carson of the Tampa FBI office who interviewed Harry Black about his involvement in the Delaware high school class reunion murders last year. His report indicated that the Tampa police knew how to find Harry.

CHAPTER SEVENTEEN

"CHARLES, IN YOUR REPORT TO William Carle of the Delaware Branch last year when you were asked to locate and interview Harry Black, you reported that the Tampa Police were very cooperative in finding Harry."

"Can you ask them to tell us where we can get in touch with him again, so we can interview him regarding another murder here in Tampa?"

"We would also appreciate your assistance in working with us on a new case involving Mr. Black. I have a cell phone number but I don't want him to know that we want to talk to him. I prefer to contact him unannounced."

"I certainly will. Nice seeing you again Bob, I will be happy to assist you in getting in touch with Harry if you wish. I found him very cooperative last year and we developed a friendship that made our investigation a lot easier. It is not easy to work with drug addicts, but Harry is an exception. He is on and off drugs constantly."

"He really would like to quit the drug business; but he is just beyond help any more. He just likes the life that he now leads and all his friends are involved with drugs.

I haven't been involved with him now since last fall; but I have contacts in the Tampa PD that I am sure can find him."

Agent Carson contacted someone in the police drug unit, and true to his comments, he had Harry's place of residence within an hour and the three agents found Harry at home in Tampa. They asked him to join them in a Burger King nearby for some talks. He agreed but wanted to go to a more distant restaurant. They found a McDonalds about a mile or two away. Harry was happy to be interviewed out of sight of his drug friends.

"Gosh, Mr. Spedden and Mr. Carson, what do you think I have done this time. Those girls in Seaford were murdered by Horace Hastings and surely that case is closed isn't it?"

"Well Harry, that was the result of the investigation at that time; but we have a reason to believe now, that someone else may have done those murders because there has been another murder up there since we last talked with you,"

"Oh dear, here we go again. Mr. Spedden, I am not involved with any murders. I haven't been in Delaware since Christmas. I have a job now. I play regularly at four different clubs here in Tampa and one in St. Pete. I am also not dealing or messing with drugs. I feel great. You got to believe me Mr. Carson. Was the girl another class mate?"

"No Harry, we don't think you are involved and the recent victim was from Blades, Delaware and not a classmate of Harriet or Jeanne. All we want is to talk to you about is of someone else who may be involved."

"Well Blades is just across the Nanticoke River from Seaford. Who do you mean Oliver Hill? I haven't seen him since I last went to Delaware. He does like women. He really did like my old companion Grace Marvel—remember?"

"Yes, I remember Grace she was your friend who died from a drug over dose. We thought Oliver was involved with that."

"Yes, but he didn't have anything to do with that."

"Yes that's right but that or Oliver is not what we want to talk to you about. We have had a report that you were seen at the Tropic Club with a man named Freddie. Do you know anyone named Freddie that you could have been seen with at the club?"

"The only Freddie I know is Fred Messick. I knew him when I was in Delaware. I think he lived in Laurel. Oh my, do you mean him? It seems you guys are always after friends of mine."

"Perhaps that is the man, we don't know. But what can you tell us about his being seen at the Tropic Club with you?"

"Well yes, I was in the Tropic to pick up my paycheck, on a Saturday afternoon and he was in there having a beer. He waved to me and I went over and he introduced himself to me. I had seen him several times at the dances where

I play; but I did not recognize him until this particular Saturday."

"You said he was a friend of yours. What can you tell me about him?"

"Well I guess he is more of an acquaintance rather than a friend. In fact, I really didn't know him too well even when I was in Delaware. He told me his name and then he asked me if I remembered him. I told him that I had seen him at the different clubs, but I did not know exactly who he was."

"He told me then that I should remember him because I had—well—had performed oral sex on him twice in Delaware, and then he told me that he was from Laurel, Delaware and gave me his name. I'm gay remember?"

"I knew that I had seen him, but I told him I didn't remember his having a bad scar like that on his forehead. He said that he fell off a ladder when painting a house and cut his head."

"He asked me if I would like to take him again, and of course, I did, and we left the club. I see him periodically at the clubs at times, but I have not been with him since that Saturday. I don't know where he lives or if he is still in the area."

"Harry, can we trust that you will not talk to him, should you see him again about what we have discussed today? He is a dangerous man."

"You know I can promise you that Mr. Carson. I still thank you for helping me get off drugs. I still have your card and I will call you on my cell phone should I see him at any of the clubs I play at."

"Thank you Harry. We are very happy that you have become clean. Keep up the good work and stay that way. I'm going to stop in some of the clubs and hear you play."

"Yes, please do that; but do not have any conversation with me. You know why. I'm off drugs, but many of those friends of mine aren't and they would drop me like a hot potato, if they knew you were FBI. I will know if you are there. I hope you enjoy what you hear."

"I understand Harry, stay clean. Oh, by the way Harry do you by chance know a girl named Mary Hendricks?

"Yes, I know Mary, or I did, word around the clubs is that she was killed. Oh—so that's it, that's why you are questioning me. But, I can tell you right now Mr. Carson I meet Mary and a group of girls about her age that frequent the clubs most every weekend and they all enjoy my music and often followed me to the different clubs where I play."

"I told them they were members of my so called fan club. They are in a group of about five or six ladies that like my style of music and follow me from club to club. The only one I ever had. Mary or one of the other girls would call me on Friday or Saturday mornings on my cell phone to inquire as to where I was playing. That's all—she was just a friend who liked my music. We talked a lot during breaks."

"That's all—her favorite song was *Misty*, and I played it every time she was in the crowd. Of course most of my music was a far cry from *Misty*. The crowds like the hip-stuff, but I got away with playing *Misty* because I always introduced it as a song for the lady of my life even though Mary or any of the girls had no interest in me personally. You haven't forgot that I'm gay have you?"

"No, I know that, you told me so last year and just a minute ago. Do you know of any men with whom Mary was friendly?"

"No, I don't ever recall any of those girls ever being with a man when they came in the clubs, except one, her name was Karen. I don't know her last name. She sort of got out of the group. Someone said that she had got married; but I never saw her with a man at any of the clubs either. If she did marry, I never saw her at a club with a man"

"Did you notice any of them ever going out of the club with any men?"

"Yes, occasionally I would see one or another of them leave the club at the end of the evening. I can't say if I ever saw Mary leave with a man and if she did I wouldn't know a name to give you."

On the way back to the station, the agents agreed that they would start having the clubs on a stake out, especially on Friday and Saturday nights, because the four girls stated that was the only time they went to the clubs. They would have several male and female FBI agents go to all the clubs where Fred normally played and Bob and Charles would definitely go to the club where Fred was playing on those nights so they could have Harry identify Fred should he come in the club.

Agent Spedden's cell phone rang and he was told that a girl's body had just been found in Taylor Park, in Largo, Florida just off of 8th Avenue SW.

She had no identification on her and she appeared to have been raped. She had been strangled with a plastic covered wire. The agents told the police that they were on the way and not to let anyone near the area until they got there by sealing off the perimeter.

"Oh, no here we go again. Just as I thought we had a good chance to nail that guy before he did this again. I do hope he doesn't take off as he usually does. I'll bet he's already on the road to a different location."

On arrival at the scene where the woman's body was found outside a car on the ground, Agent Spedden asked the police officers, if they had made any identification on the girl yet.

He was told that a woman's purse was found in the car that was parked nearby. There was no money except change in her wallet. Her credit cards were not taken. They were certain that this was her purse when they compared her face to that found on the Florida driver's license.

The name on the license was Gladys Hill and that her address was in Tampa. She was 22 years old.

Bob took one look at the wire around the girl's neck and knew immediately that Fred Messick had killed another girl. She was partially naked and it was assumed that she had indeed been raped. She was left in a sitting position against a tree. She was placed there in an intentional sexually provocative position.

Charles mentioned, "Well Fred is really getting 'kinky'—he is now staging all his victims in different positions."

Bob answered, "What possible jollies can a guy get on staging his victims in such explicit positions?"

"I really don't know, but there was a serial murderer here in Central and North Florida a year or so back, who did the same thing. He raped and murdered only college girls. He got in their dormitory rooms. Do you remember that case?"

"Oh yeah, I remember that now. I saw a few of the pictures—absolutely disgusting. I wonder if the psychologists ever made a study of why serial rapists kill and do those strange things."

"Bill Carle and I were talking about that recently, and he said that he thought that the guy who did that to the college girls, did it because he took pictures of his victims and when they arrested the guy, he had over twenty pictures of different girls in his car.

They said those pictures helped them solve a dozen or more rapes and murders that they had never connected him to. Can you imagine a guy killing over twenty people?"

"Yes I can, it seems we are chasing such a character every few years. At the rate Fred is killing them he will be in that group pretty soon himself. You know Charles, what I can't get over with this killer is that he was once engaged to be married. Why did he not want to rape and kill her?"

"Bob didn't he eventually did rape and kill her?"

"Oh yes, I knew that, I just forgot but he didn't kill her until after he had killed several girls. I just wonder what it is that creates a serial killer. Something happened to Fred though, because he didn't stage his early victims that we know about."

"I think they go insane. He did use the wire on all of them as if he wanted us to know that he had killed them. It's like he wants a trade mark."

"I agree to that, they have to be insane. What we rarely find out in cases such as this, is the actual total number of victims, robberies, and other killings that they must do to keep themselves in funds—those that are never connected to the killer."

"Well we do occasionally connect a few robberies and even a few murders that were connected to serial killers; but you are right I am sure that most of them are never connected."

A police officer who was conducting a search of the area, called the detective who was heading up the investigation and reported, "You better get over here. I have found another body."

This body was of a young man who also was partially naked and he had been shot in the upper back.

In a car found parked at the site, the police found his pants. His wallet was found on the ground outside the car. The car's front doors were both open and blood was all over the car's interior. It was evident that the man had been shot in his back while in the car and that he had managed to drag himself from the car about 50 feet where he died.

His driver's license found in the wallet listed his name as Philip Webster, age 23, and his residence as being in Tampa, Florida. There was no money in his wallet. Also found in the car was a bottle of whiskey, two paper cups, and a small packet of what appeared to be a drug of some sort.

Bob told agents Carson and O'Neal, "Well this murder is different from all of the previous rapes and murder we have linked to Fred Messick because there are two victims and one of the victims was killed by a gun, and the second victim, is a man."

"We were just talking about other crimes that a serial killer commits that are usually not known but here we have one in front of us that can be connected. I am confident that Fred is the killer of this girl, and this man. Why he persists on using that wire cable, is beyond me. It appears as if he wants us to know that he is the one killing these girls."

"It certainly appears that way; but as we were told in our training, it is not unusual for a serial killer to take steps to do just that. I was looking at the victim's neck, and it doesn't appear to have any markings that are usually found on a strangulation case."

"I'm not an expert in forensic investigations; but I would almost bet that this girl was raped and died from strangulation by the killers own hands. If you look close the wire has no signs of tension around her neck. I bet it was placed there by the killer purposely. The girl is also covered with blood and did you note that she was not staged in a sexually explicit position as his last few victims were."

"It does look like that to me too Bob, what do you think is the reason that he did not follow his usual staging?"

"My opinion on this murder, at the moment, is that this man and woman were parked here in the city park, probably drinking and taking drugs, and were preparing to have sex or were in the act, when the killer shot the male in the back."

"Then the woman was pulled out of the car and raped and killed. I suspect that during the time he was raping the girl that the male victim crawled to where he was found dead. I think that when her lover was shot she was splattered with his blood from the gun shot."

And she surely was not a pretty sight after that. I think he didn't want her picture, or didn't want to remember her in such a condition. He may not have even raped her. What do you think of my assessment?"

"Well I certainly think that is exactly what happened. I think we should look to see if we can find any other fresh tire tracks around here. I suspect that Fred drove here and found the couple parked."

On their return to police headquarters, Bob called special agent Bill Carle at the FBI branch office in Wilmington, Delaware and gave him a full report of the incident as well as his thoughts on what had happened.

"Bob, you better check on the drug type etc. Ask the coroner if there are traces of whiskey or drugs in the bodies, get the caliber of the bullet and have the bullet itself sent to headquarters to see if its characteristics match any murder cases that are still open by gunshot of that caliber. Maybe even some robberies."

The Chief of Police's secretary gave Bob a message that he had a call come in on the chief's office phone for him when the chief was out of the office. Bob closed his conversation with Bill and read the message to the investigating team after reading it himself.

"Men, I have a note here from Harry Black. Harry lives here in Tampa and we interviewed him a few days ago. I had given him a card to contact me if our suspect was seen at any of the clubs where he plays music. He said he did not have my card with him, and that is why he called the city police."

"He said that Fred Messick had come into Rachel's and was at the bar drinking but he left shortly after coming in. He was alone when he left the club."

"Bob told the men, find out from the coroner, the estimated date and time the victims were killed. I would guess last night, because this park has a lot of visitors during the day."

"Agent Carson and I are going to contact Harry and see if we can find anything helpful. Agent O'Neal will contact the family of the victims, if they can be found, to determine when they were last seen. I am guessing; but I would almost bet, that Harry followed this couple out of the club. Maybe Harry can tell us if the couple was at the club."

After reaching Harry, He agreed to meet them at the same McDonalds as before.

Bob told Harry, "You just have to have a sandwich and a milkshake to talk with us don't you?"

"That's a small price to pay for the information I have for you."

"Just kidding Harry, what's the information you have for us?"

"Just this, shortly before I called you at police headquarters, Fred Messick came into the club on Tyler Street, and went to the bar and was having a few drinks. He was alone but was flirting with many of the women. He danced with a few of them. Like you had instructed me, I was observing to see if he seemed to be attracted to any particular woman, and I noticed him talking to this one woman who was trying to ignore him."

"After a man who I suspect was her boyfriend or husband came to the table and sat down with her, Fred went quickly back to the bar."

"I was hoping that I could contact you because he was at the bar for over an hour and I saw him leave the club as soon as the couple left the club. I think he was following them. I wish I had the card you gave me. I had left it at home."

"Thank you Harry, if I bring you a few pictures of some women, do you think that you could identify the girl he was trying to talk with?"

"I'm sure I can, but don't ask me when I am at the club."

"Oh yeah, another Big Mac and fries I suppose will do it."

"You got it right."

Arrangements were made for Harry to meet them again at the same McDonalds. The picture of the woman found raped and murdered in Taylor Park was identified by Harry as soon as it was shown to him.

"Yes, that's the girl. I have seen her at the club many times and the man is the one that came and sat down with her."

Chapter Eighteen

THE STAKEOUTS AT THE CLUBS where Harry played failed to find Fred at any of the clubs. After two weeks the male and female agents were taken from the clubs, and Harry was given a cell phone that was programmed to contact the FBI Headquarters in Tampa with a simple one push of a button.

After pushing the call button, he was instructed to push the buttons 3343 only if he saw Fred in any of the clubs. He would not have to talk on the phone. The phone was programmed to give the FBI information immediately at which one of the clubs Harry was in when the buttons were pushed.

A test at each of five clubs that Harry was playing music at the time was conducted and the system was found to be operational in all the clubs. The phone was also capable of being used for his regular calls both incoming and outgoing. It was hoped that Harry would have it with him at all times.

Three weeks had past and there were no sightings of Fred. The investigating team feared that Fred had moved off to another location, as he always did in the past. There had also been no rapes or murders in Pinellas or Hillsborough counties.

Their fears were correct. There had been no rapes or murders in the area and Fred had not been seen in any of the clubs that he was known to have gone to in the past.

Special Agent William Clarke pulled his men back to Wilmington, Delaware and once again in less than a week after he recalled the teams, he received word from the FBI Headquarters in Washington, that there had been four rapes that ended with the murder of the rape victims in the States of Alabama and Arkansas and each of the murders had a resemblance to those committed by Fred Messick.

He was instructed to dispatch his team to Alabama where the last three rapes and murders was committed. They were all to report to the Biloxi Police Department in the Mississippi branch office where a command center was to be established. After setting up the office he was to dispatch a few agents to Little Rock, Arkansas where three rapes and murders had been committed. It was thought that Fred was no longer in Arkansas and was thought to be in Alabama or perhaps on his way back to Florida.

After the team developed its' plan of operations two agents were sent to Little Rock to check out the three cases there. The remaining team was to concentrate on Mobile, Alabama and to attempt to prevent any additional rapes or murders should Fred still be that city.

Biloxi was a military town and had a lot of bars and young people dancing facilities, similar to those Fred was known to attend.

Once again Bob Spedden was placed in charge of the operation and he arrived in Biloxi, Mississippi with his team of five agents.

He requested that the Little Rock, office send him copy of the files on the three cases in Arkansas so the team could review the files with the entire team before they left to make their inquiries in Little Rock. The remaining three agents would setup surveillance in the leading bars and clubs that catered to dancers and young adults. It was now well known that Fred was frequenting these types of businesses.

Based on the fact that the third body found in Arkansas was found over six days ago, the sheriff said that he thought there was a real possibility that the killer had indeed left Arkansas and was now possibly in the Mobile area.

Back in Little Rock interviews with all known friends of the three girls in Little Rock were scheduled and two of the girls were known to have attended popular bars, or clubs in that city, and ironically both of those two had frequented the same club the very night that they disappeared.

This information was relayed to the team in Biloxi, so that their attention could be directed to those same types of clubs in Biloxi that were in Tampa where additional agents were sent out of the Orlando, Florida office.

The team felt confident that if Fred was to visit any such club in those cities they would be there.

Bob told the Sheriff on the telephone that he was confident, based on Fred's past habit of moving on after several murders that Fred was most likely out of Alabama and was probably on his way back to Florida. That is why they set up the control center in Biloxi where they could rapidly respond to all three cities. In the past Fred always reappeared in Florida after having raped and murdered a few women elsewhere.

Agent Carson was sent to Little Rock to work with the agents on the cases there and Bob went on to Mobile.

On their arrival in Mobile, The county Sheriff told the team that another body had just been discovered early that very morning and the Coroner estimated that the date of death had been no more than a matter of hours before he arrived at the scene.

Bob was excited this was the first murder that they had been tracking where the body was less than two or three days old. That may prove to be helpful to them.

Now that there was a fresh body of a victim they felt sure the murderer was still in the area. They had to work fast.

"I am certain these are all by Fred; but, we have not established yet that these new murders were actually committed by Fred Messick. Could we have copies of all of your findings?"

"Certainly, but the body we found late this morning is still where it was found. I instructed all of my men to seal off the area pending your arrival, so we have nothing to report on this murder except to say that it was discovered by a man with the Park's maintenance crew just a little over two hours ago."

"One of the maintenance men is reported to have witnessed a man standing over the body from the road level above where the body was found. He was replacing light bulbs in the roadway's overhead lights."

"The body was found in one of the picnic areas early this morning. I am prepared to have you taken there as soon as you are ready."

"That's great, let's get out there right away so we can have a good look before dark and can you have that maintenance man meet us there. I am very anxious to hear what he saw or heard."

"Yes, that can be arranged I will have the Park Ranger bring him to the area."

A search of the area was already underway when the sheriff and Bob and two of his agents arrived at the scene. Bob was taken to the body which was covered with a yellow plastic sheet.

The sheet was removed and Bob immediately recognized the wire cable around the young ladies neck. He made a note and was surprised that unlike the last six victims this lady was not staged in Fred's usual sexual scenes.

Bob wondered why. He thought that possibly he had discovered that there was a witness to this murder. He was hoping that was the case.

The Park Ranger arrived with Sam Fulton. Sam was the park's maintenance man and Bob introduced himself.

"Mr. Fulton, I am Robert Spedden a special agent of the Federal Bureau of Investigation. I have been assigned the duties to obtain the facts regarding the murder that was committed here in the Park early this morning. I have been told that you witnessed a man standing over the women this morning. Is that true?"

"Yes that is true Mr. Spedden; but I did not know at the time that it was a murder. I saw the woman lying on the ground and this man standing over her. I thought that she was sick or something."

"You said that the man was standing over her."

"Yes he was standing between me and the woman and he was blocking most of my view of the woman. I didn't know that she was naked until I arrived in that area a few minutes later."

"What time was it that you first saw them?"

"It would have been about 4:00 o'clock in the morning, I was on the midnight shift this morning."

"What were you doing at that hour of the night?"

"My job is to see that the rest rooms are all cleaned, paper supplies are ample, and to repair anything that is left on a work order for me to do by the Park Ranger who is in charge of the Park. This morning I was asked to check all of the overhead lights and replace any light bulbs that were out. That is what I was doing when I saw the couple below."

"What do you mean by below?"

"Well we have a fork lift that lifts me up to the fixtures about fifteen feet up. I was on the road up there which is on a higher level road then where we are now."

Pointing up to the road above he said, "See what I mean?"

"I was having trouble getting the shade off that fixture up there and I looked down and I could see them down thru the trees. I was in the basket."

"Do you think that the man saw you up there?"

"I don't think so, but if he did he didn't look my way as far as I remember. He was still there when I got back in my truck."

"I decided that I would go check on them to see if they needed help and I drove down to the end of the road and went down the camp road into the camping area. When I got there I passed him going out of the camp ground and I assumed that all was okay; but I had to go on down because you can't turn around on the road."

"When I got down to the camp area, that's when I saw the woman in my headlights and I went right to the phone and called the police."

"Did you get a look at the man?"

"No, it was still dark."

"Was he in a car?"

"No it was a Van and there was some printing on the front door, but I didn't or couldn't read what it was. I think it was an old Dodge Van."

"Could you make out what color the van was?"

"I'm not real sure, it was still dark, but I think it might have been white. I was trying to look at him in the van as I went past him so I could ask him if all was okay, but he turned his head away from me."

"Does the Park allow people in the park at any time?"

"Not really, except in the camping area because there's a fee to use that area, but I see them in the picnic area there all the time. It's like a lover's lane in the summer but at this time of the year few people come down here. It's the Park Ranger's job to handle that and collect the fees."

"Of course after ten o'clock they quit making their rounds."

"Well Mr. Fulton, I thank you for the information and we may be back in touch with you later."

Agent Spedden gave all his agents on the various teams the description of Fred's van as described by Mr. Fulton and they were looking for white vans at all the various dancing clubs. He alerted the Florida team in Tampa that Fred was possibly on his way back to Florida.

Fred Messick was aware that he was seen at the scene of his last rape and murder. As he was preparing the victim for taking her picture, he heard a noise on the park road which was about 30 feet higher than the campground where he was.

How foolish he had been to have done this in such an open area. He was certain that he had been seen and that he must get out of the park at once.

He got in his van and drove up the campground road to the park road and passed the work truck coming down Camp Ground Road as he left the area. He turned his head in a direction away from the driver of the truck and left the park at a high rate of speed.

He decided that he had to dispose of his van immediately he hoped that he could locate another vehicle quickly.

At this hour of the morning he knew that the auto rental firms would still be closed and that the authorities would soon be checking all such rental firms if they got a description of his van and he was certain that they had that information now.

He decided to abandon the van at once. He saw a blue H sign ahead of him and realized that would be a great place to abandon the van. He pulled into the hospital parking lot, and removed from the van, a few items including the revolver he used in his robberies, some cartridges, some pictures, and his camera.

He saw nothing that would help the authorities find him and left the key in the switch. He entered the hospital and went in the cafeteria where he had a breakfast.

After breakfast he left the hospital and caught the first city bus that arrived at the hospital's bus stop. He had no idea where the bus would take him. He just wanted to be away from the area. When he got off the bus he hailed a cab and asked to be taken to the Greyhound bus terminal. He bought a ticket to Nashville, Tennessee where he spent the night at a nearby Day's Inn.

For the first time since killing Harriet and Jeanne in Delaware he was scared. He knew that the newspapers were now showing pictures of him. He wondered where they got those pictures, but quickly determined that they got the photograph from his driver's license.

He had to change his looks. He bought a pair of clear glass eyeglasses and quit shaving and let his hair grow. His money was running low and he knew that he would have to do a few robberies soon.

CHAPTER NINETEEN

FRED'S VAN WAS FOUND IN the hospital parking lot after eight days. The FBI agent's ride through known dance bars parking lots looking for a white van was discontinued.

Fred was in hiding and everything was in a wait and see again. Fred no longer had his wire as it was left in his van. He was avoiding the Tampa area.

The FBI, issued a notice about the wire to all its' branch offices along with a statement that all rapes and murders in the future were to be reported to headquarters until such time as a new habitual clue could be used to tie the rapes and murders to Fred.

Fred was still in Nashville, and had found a job painting for a building contractor that was building a large new condo complex. He was assured of work for a minimum of six months. He was now using his middle name and had a bank account in the name of F William Messick and soon had a credit card, a Tennessee driver's license, and a new pickup truck, all in that name.

His hair was now much longer but was well trimmed. His glasses were wide framed and hid most of the scar on his eyebrow. He had found a few friends and was once again attending some of the area clubs and dance bars. He had not been with a woman now for over six months

He visited a boat dealership and bought a 50 foot length of red nylon 3/8th inch anchor rope. This would serve his needs.

Two days later a girl's body was found in a wooded area adjacent to a city golf course. She had been strangled with a red nylon rope and her body was staged in a sexual explicit position.

In a few days agent William Clarke in Wilmington Delaware was given a report on that murder and was asked to determine if this victim could possibly have been a victim of Fred Messick. The staging position of the body was thought to be a copy cat of Fred's victims.

Bill Clarke asked Bob to take a look at this murder and Bob went to Nashville to review the transcripts. He got his answer on the second day after arriving in Nashville when another girl's body was found strangled with a red anchor rope and placed in a similar sexually explicit position.

Bob was certain that Fred was active again. The Nashville police had learned that both girls were last seen at a local dance bar and that both girls had left the bars alone, and each of the girl's car was found in the bar's parking lot, and for the first time this most prominent club had images on a tape of the girl leaving the club, but it failed to show what happened to her after she was out of the camera's view.

There were pictures of a man leaving the bar shortly after the girl, but he too went out of the camera's view area. Bob asked his headquarters to examine the few pictures that they had, to see if they could prepare a statement as to the height, weight, race, etc. for a description of the man photographed.

The report fell within the known characteristics of Fred Messick, the photo report stated that the man now had hair, well groomed and that he wore dark rimmed eyeglasses.

Bob then requested that the lab take the photo they had of Fred from his South Carolina driver's license and to change his hair to match that on this new photo, with dark rimmed glasses. In two days he had a new generated likeness of Fred Messick.

The new photo was disseminated to the teams investigating the deaths of the two Nashville girls, and three out of seven bartenders in the bars when asked if they had seen the man, stated that they had indeed seen such a man in their bars, and that he was a frequent customer.

The created photo's were distributed to dance bars in Alabama, Tennessee, Georgia, Mississippi, and Florida and Bob hand delivered a copy of the photo to Harry Black in Tampa to study but did not leave it with Harry.

"Harry, we have a feeling that Fred Messick has changed his appearance to look like this photo. I am giving you once again the special cell phone that we had prepared for you. Do you remember how to work it?"

"I think so, but what were the four numbers I have to push 33 something, I think?"

"Yes that's it 3343—just push those four numbers and forget it. We will be there in a matter of minutes."

Bob was right in his hunch that Fred was back in Tampa. Fred arrived in Tampa a week later and visited the Tropic Bar the following night.

Harry studied this bearded man and convinced himself that he was indeed Fred Messick.

Then Harry punched in 3343 on the cell phone between musical songs and the signal that Fred was in the Club Tropic was sent.

Five agents were on their way to the club within minutes, one of which was Agent Bob Spedden.

All exits from the club were being observed by the FBI as Bob entered the club. He went directly to the bar and chose a stool from which he could see the entire area. Harry used his head to show him where Fred was seated.

Harry removed his cell phone from his pocket again and pushed the buttons 3343 again that alerted the agents outside that the suspect had been sighted and agent Carson entered the club and approached agent Spedden still seated at the bar.

They then approached the booth where Fred and a young lady were seated and in a flash Bob grabbed Fred and with the help of agent Carson had him handcuffed. Three other agents entered the building and Fred and the girl with him were taken to the Police Department in handcuffs.

A call was made to William Carle in Wilmington, Delaware at the FBI Branch Office and he was on his way to Tampa out of the Philadelphia airport that same evening.

A decision was made between the different officials that Fred would be tried in the Florida courts where they had the strongest case against him and the fact that he was in Florida when arrested.

After his arrival in Tampa agent Carle from Delaware requested to interview the suspect, Fred Messick and arrangements were made at the Police Headquarters in Tampa.

"First Fred, allow me to introduce myself I am William Carle, an agent of the Federal Bureau of Investigation. I have been assigned to the cases for which you are accused of being the suspect in those murders and rapes. I would like to ask you a few questions that may help us in our investigation.

By law, I must advise you of your rights and I want you to know that we are seeking information only.

Carle read him his rights and proceeded with the interview after Fred had acknowledged orally that he had been given his rights.

"Fred, of course the first question I have for you is— did you rape and murder, Mary Hendricks of Tampa some months ago?"

"I don't know any girl named Mary Hendricks."

"How about those two girls Harriet O'Brien and Jeanne Records up in Seaford, Delaware did you rape and murder them.

"I don't know any girls with those names. I don't want to tell you anything that you don't know."

"Fred, we know you have committed several murders in several states that have the death panel. Your only hope now is that a judge and jury will not ask for the death penalty and for that to be possible, your cooperation with us on putting an end to any open cases, would be the best thing you can hope for in getting them to drop the death penalty. While I cannot guarantee you any leniency, I am certain that your only hope will be how you cooperate with us in putting to rest any of our unsolved murders."

"Fred, as your state of Florida appointed defense lawyer, Mr. Spedden speaks the truth and I urge you to cooperate in answering his questions truthfully. It will be much easier for me to prepare a defense with you later. If any question will hurt our case, I will stop you from answering."

"I do want to co-operate Mr. Spedden, really I do."

"Thank you Fred, now let us get down to the facts again. Did you rape and kill Mary Hendricks last week in Taylor Park in Largo?"

"I didn't know her name, but yes, I did rape and kill a girl in Taylor Park in Largo some time ago."

Was Harriet O'Brien in Seaford, Delaware the first girl that you ever raped and killed?"

"I didn't say that I raped a girl name Harriet O'Brien."

"Did you rape and kill two girls in Seaford last year?"

"Yes and no. I raped and killed a girl in Seaford, her name was Jeanne, but I did not rape the other girl but I did kill her."

"Fred her name was Harriet O'Brien."

Bob handed Fred a list of his suspected rape and murder victims.

"Fred you murdered every one of the women on this list. If you didn't rape Harriet then why did you kill her?"

"I did intend to rape her; but she told me that she was pregnant and she would give me oral sex if I did not rape her. I had never had a woman give me oral sex before, so I took her up on her offer."

"Then why did you kill her?"

"Because I was about to marry a girl up there in Delaware and I was afraid that she would find out about what I had done. I wasn't sure if she knew me or not. I did know that I had seen her many times when we were in high school. She was a great basketball player. I killed her so she would not be able to identify me."

"Was this your first victim to be killed?"

"Yes, it was."

"Then a few days later did you rape and kill Jeanne Records?"

"Yes, I did both of those things."

"Then why did you rape and kill Jeanne if you had already killed Harriet so she wouldn't tell anyone and your fear that your fiancé would find out. Weren't you just getting in deeper all the time?"

"Yes, I was, but Jennifer, who I was engaged to marry, had just refused to go to Florida with me, and I just didn't give a damn at that time. I went to Florida alone. I killed Jeanne for the same reason. I was afraid that she may have known who I was."

"Fred we have been told that you were once engaged to be married to Jennifer Collins of Laurel, Delaware. Is that true, and what can you tell me about her?"

"Jennifer is the only girl that I ever really loved. She is the one I just told you that I was engaged to. I dated her many times. We never had sex either. I can't explain why but she was the first girl that approached me for a date. She was the one that came on to me. We went to ball games together, to the movies, we enjoyed being together and she was the love of my life."

"She was the first and only girl that ever told me she loved me. I just never had an urge to rape her. I surely did want to have sex with her but she always told me that we should wait until we were married. I always wanted to please her and never would have forced myself on her. I think that is the reason I never raped her. I did love her so."

"But you did eventually rape and kill her didn't you?"

"Yes but not until I found out she was going to marry another man a year later. In fact, that is why I went back to Delaware. I was going to try and win her back. She wanted nothing to do with me so then I became determined to have her. That is when I raped and killed her."

"Fred, let's get back to when you left Seaford the first time for Florida after killing Harriet and Jeanne."

"Oh yeah, I was not getting enough work painting in and around Seaford, so I decided to go south where there was work all year around. Jennie would not go with me and I was upset with that decision."

"I turned to Harriet and used her to take my frustrations out on. I just told you about what happened and then I turned to Jeanne and after all the activity of the police on those murders, I decided that I had better get out of town because my breakup with Jennie might be considered by the police, as a reason to rape and kill Harriet and Jeanne, and that really was the reason."

"So you went south. Did you go then to St. Petersburg or Tampa?"

"No, I got as far as North Carolina. I went to a bar and got drunk. I mean really drunk. I knew that I had really messed up what life I had. A prostitute came over to my table and we eventually went to her room. I was so upset with myself that I paid the girl $25.00 for nothing I had no desire for sex. I now wish that I had had sex with her because maybe that would have satisfied my urge to have sex and perhaps that could have stopped me from raping girls."

"Instead I just wanted nothing to do with a whore. It seems now that I only want sex when I have to fight for it."

"Why do you always kill the girl after you have sex?"

"I really can't answer that question. I suppose it has something to do with my wanting to take pictures of all the girls I rape. It gives me a high that I can't explain. A feeling of power I suppose, and that high lasts for about a week. Then it all stops,
I get depressed and sick thinking of what I have done. I would have done anything to end the rapes and the killing but before I knew it the urge to rape a girl always came back and I just couldn't fight it. I keep the urge in check by looking at my pictures."

"Oh, is that the reason that you always sit them in sexual explicit poses?"

"Yeah, I guess that has something to do with it."

"Tell me Fred, do you always kill all of the girls you rape?"

"Oh no, many of the girls quit fighting and submit. If I feel they don't know anything about me I often let them live. But sometimes there would be something special about one of them and I would want to save their picture, so I have to kill them so I can take their picture."

"Don't you ever regret raping or killing any of these girls?"

"Yes, I do many times; but I just can't stop myself from doing it."

"Fred, some people think that you go in and out of insanity. Do you think that you are insane?"

"Hold up Fred, Don't answer that question it might affect our case in the future."

"That's right Fred, you don't have to answer my questions and if your attorney says not to answer then you should do as he says. Can I continue?"

"Yes."

"Good boy Fred. Can you give us any information on any girls that you have not killed after you raped them?"

"Perhaps that would be a lot of help to us in closing any open rape cases we have. I am sure that a judge or jury would look favorably on you if our report stated that you cooperated with us in resolving these cases."

Fred's lawyer shook his head favorable for Fred that it was okay to answer that question.

"Well I can tell you one such instance. It was in Daytona Beach. I was on the beach looking for a prospect when I met this beautiful girl. I knew that she was young but I didn't realize that she was as young as she was. We got to talking and before long she agreed to go with me to get a pizza. After eating the pizza I parked the car with her in a wooded area."

"I asked her if she had ever had sex before and she said that she had not but all of her best friends had. I asked her if she would like to experience a sex act, and she said no, she told me she might get pregnant. I lied and told her that I had protection. She still refused so I raped her. I knew that she did not know anything about me, so I did not kill her."

"A day or two later, I read about the girl being raped and found out that she was only fourteen years old. Mr. Spedden, I really did regret having done that. I couldn't sleep for several nights without feeling mad at myself for ruining that girl's life, and I even wondered if she would get pregnant."

"Didn't you tell her that you had protection?"

"Yes but I had to rape her, so I didn't use it."

Chapter Twenty

"AFTER THAT I WENT ON to Tampa and about a month or so later I went to a club for a drink and I found a guy there playing in the band that I knew when he lived in Delaware. His name was Harry Black. He told me that he played in the band at three or four clubs in that area."

"Did you go to any of them?"

"Oh yes, I first met him at the Tropic Club. I then went several times to Rachael's Club, and once to the club in St. Petersburg. I forgot its' name. That was not as nice as the other clubs he went to."

"Did you meet a girl named Helen Reeves in any of the clubs?"

"So you know about her too. I was sure that I would not be charged with her death."

"Yes, we connected you to her because you used the same type of wire to strangle her. We put out a question across the land for a listing of unresolved murders in which that type of wire was used."

"The police in St. Petersburg gave us the file on Helen. Tell me how did you entice her to get in your car before you raped and killed her?"

"That was easy, she had come to the club unescorted, had a few too many drinks, and I offered to take her home."

"But the report that I got indicated that she was found naked but had not been raped. Why did you kill her if you didn't rape her?"

"When I got parked, she drunkenly told me that she had wanted to meet me. She also told me that my name was Fred and that scared me because I could probably be traced to her if she ever told anyone about me. I knew then that she would have to be killed."

"When I was ready to have sex with her, she passed out and there she was lying naked on a blanket I had placed on the ground easy for the taking, but having sex with a drunken girl who was passed out just did not appeal to me. I enjoy the fight for the sex. She could give me no fight at all. She had beautiful tits and a beautiful body; but I am certain that if she had not passed out, she would have given me sex without my having to rape her. She was indeed a pretty girl. I strangled her and then masturbated over her."

"Tell me Fred couldn't you have satisfied yourself by paying a prostitute for your sex urges and eliminated all these murders over the years?"

"No I couldn't Mr. Spedden. I really can't tell you why because I really don't know why, but I have had sex with many girls over the years and have had sex with several prostitutes; but unless I force myself on a girl, it just doesn't satisfy me at all. With me it is the fight that arouses me."

"I see. Fred, the next girl we have on our list is Betty Hopkins who was raped and murdered up in Gainesville. What can you tell me about her?"

"So that's her name. I did rape and kill a girl up there around Christmas. I never did read about that murder in the papers because I was on my way up North to Delaware."

"I stopped at a shopping center there to get a sub sandwich from a Publix store and as I parked, I saw this beautiful lady taking her groceries out of a cart and putting them in her car right next to me. The wind was blowing and when she leaned over to put some items in her car the wind blew her skirt up and it got caught in the cart basket somehow."

"I approached her and asked if she needed any help. Of course she said she didn't. I opened my car door and hit her on the head with a crowbar that I kept in my car and I pushed her into my car and drove off and parked in a secluded area. The girl was not dead and she was unconscious. I raped her and I then strangled her and took her picture."

"I remember that girl well, because she was the first girl that I had ever hit hard enough to knock her out. I didn't enjoy doing that. She didn't fight me. I got sick when I looked at her picture later and I threw the picture of her away."

"I was in Gainesville because I had read in the Seaford Leader weekly newspaper, that I still got at my Tampa address, a story in the so-called society column, that my ex-fiancé Jennifer Collins was about to get married."

"I was heading up to Delaware. I was hoping; but knowing my chances in getting her back was zero. But I was determined to try. I know that she loved me at the time we broke up. I have never really got over losing her. I just regret that I made a bad decision when I left her years ago. I was hoping that if she would marry me, perhaps I could have put an end to my need to rape and kill."

"Mr. Spedden, I never intended to kill any of the girls I raped. When the sex was over, I can't explain why, but I just had the urge to finalize the act by killing them. The only exception to that was with the drunken girl in Taylor Park in Largo. I wanted to kill her simply because she ruined my whole evening by passing out on me."

"So Fred, that takes us back to Delaware where you killed the girl you still loved, Jennifer Collins. You did kill her even if you did still love her didn't you? Tell us about that rape and murder."

"Yes, that is the only the second rape and murder where I was sad instead of happy immediately after it was all over. Like you said, I did still love her and when I got to Seaford, I found that she still worked at the Flagship restaurant. I went there on the evening as soon as I got there."

"Where was the place you met her Fred?"

"I met her where she worked, at the Flagship Restaurant. She was on duty behind the bar. I tried to talk to her there but some bastard kept hitting on her, like she was an easy pick up, but Jennifer was anything but that. I tried to get her attention but that fool kept telling me to get lost."

"We had a few nasty remarks, but he was a big brute and no match for me, so I left. I knew that she used to get off work after one in the morning so, I waited until after one o'clock and called her on her cell phone. I still had her number in my cell phone. I was able to talk her into meeting me at the parking lot at the hospital in Seaford. Reluctantly she did."

"She met me at the lot and I got out of my truck and got in her car. We talked for well over an hour and she would not agree to break her engagement with some guy up in Alaska, I knew that I was fighting a losing battle and I got the urge to take her and have the sex that she had always denied me."

"The rest is history, I raped her and killed her and took her body to the Island in my truck, to make it look like she had been killed there. I went back to Laurel where I had been staying with an old friend for several days and one evening I saw a girl getting in her car at the grocery store, I forced her into my truck took her to the State Park called Trap Pond where I raped her and killed her like I did all the others."

"I read in the paper the next day that her name was Rosalie Ellis. I will never forget her name, because the paper said that she was married and had a child. I was deeply hurt when I read that, and I left that day to head back to Florida, where you caught up with me."

"Thank you Fred, we do appreciate your cooperation. You have cleared up a lot of questions that we had on some of these murders and it will be a relief to the families of the victims to know just what happened to their daughters."

"Thank you. I guess that is all I can do for them now. Mr. Spedden, I honestly did try to stop the killings, every time I did one, I swore that was the last one and then without any reason, the urge just kept coming back. I'm sick about it."

"One last question Fred, how come you killed the man who was with the girl named Isabel Hill who you just said you raped and killed. You shot him in the back. You didn't strangle him with the wire like you did all your other victims. Why was that?"

"That couple were parked in Taylor Park. I don't know what prompted me to ride through the park that night but I did, and I saw a couple parked in an area that I was told was a perfect "Lover's Lane.""

"I sat there for about 15 minutes or so drinking a bottle of beer and watching them smooching away. They were oblivious to my being parked about 50 or so yards from them. They both got out of their car and the man took off his shoes, pants and underwear and the girl took everything off that she had on. Her blouse and bra were already off."

"They got back in their car, and I had a throbbing erection and took my gun from my glove compartment and went over to their car and shot the man in the back. I pulled him off the girl and let him fall to the ground."

"I then pulled the girl out of the car and raped her. When I was finished I noticed that the man with her had dragged himself up the road a short distance. I discovered that he was dead when I went to make sure he was dead and I then killed the girl."

"I might add, so you can tell the head shrinks, who are trying to figure us perverts out that was the best rape I ever experienced—pleasure wise. I think that was because I really had to exert a lot of force to rape her. I have never had to kill a man before. I had pulled a gun on men in the past, when making a robbery, but I never had to kill anyone I robbed with the gun."

"You asked why I didn't use the wire on him. Well, I didn't want to fight him. In fact I never even saw his face."

"Fred you have told us about the girls on our list where we knew you were the killer. We are confident that there were others. Just how many women have you raped and killed?"

"I have raped over 20 women, 23 to be exact counting the three girls when I was a teenager in West Virginia. I have only killed nine of them."

"We know of only six of them. Will you tell us about the 3 others you killed so we can close those cases as well?"

"Yes, I will but I don't keep a record and may not remember all the details about them. I do keep the number and it is definitely 23. I do have pictures that may help me identify some of them but I don't have pictures of all of them."

Chapter Twenty One

FRED TOLD THEM THAT THE three women that were not on their list that he killed were all in Florida.

One was in Orlando and he found out after he got her in his pickup he found out she was a prostitute. He said he did not rape her but strangled her with his usual wire but that he removed the wire so that he would not be connected to her.

"I didn't want to be connected to a dirty whore." He said that he disposed of her body in the Green Swamp west of Orlando. I never saw any article in the paper about her being missing. I assume the alligators in the swamp took care of her body."

The other two women were raped and killed in the Miami area. He had pictures of both of them and the pictures were sent to the Dade county sheriff's office. They were identified and were on their missing persons lists. They were both teenagers. Fred told them that he met both girls in the same club down there and one of them was a Hispanic.

Unlike any of the other women that he had killed, Fred said he buried both of these women in shallow graves near each other.

"Are you saying that you raped and killed both of them at the same time?"

"No not at the same time. They were close friends. I had seen them in the club many times. I offered to take the first girl home and after I raped and killed her, I buried her in a wooded area west of Miami."

"I met the other girl in the same club the following week and she approached me and was telling me that her friend was not answering her calls because her phone was disconnected and she wondered if I knew where she was or where she went. She told me that she knew that she had left the club with me the previous Friday night."

"I was real upset about that, I had thought that I had left the club alone and not with the girl. I was unaware that anyone had seen us leaving the club together."

"I told her that I had not seen her since the night the three of us were at the club that week before. I asked her if she knew where the other girl lived and she said that she did."

"I was anxious to get rid of this witness. I had been careless in having been seen leaving the club with her. I offered to drive her to her friend's house so she could check on her saying that maybe she had not paid her telephone bill. She agreed."

"I now had this witness in my car. I drove her instead to the same spot that I had raped and killed the first girl. Their names were Ruth and Emily, I think. I don't remember which name was the first"

"Why did you bury these girls, you never did that in the past?"

"In the past I always left the area but I was having fun in Miami and I didn't want to go away. I buried them, because I didn't want anyone to find them and then have you guys on my tail. I know that a lot of people down there knew that I had known these girls and I didn't want you guys to know that I was in Miami."

Fred refused to go into details on any of the girls that he claimed to have raped but did not kill. He said, "I think its best that we just let those cases stay unidentified I don't want them to relive those incidents. They have probably forgotten all about it by now, but I can tell you that they were all in Florida except two who were in Georgia."

"I might add that they submitted to me without a fight after I threatened them with a knife. They were all pretty girls and all I did was threaten to cut up their faces. They all were strangers to me and I knew that I could not be connected to them. I always left the area."

"The magic word for those girls was when I mentioned cutting up their faces if they didn't submit. Of course I never told them that until after their fight that turned me on."

Bob convinced Fred to talk to a group of special FBI agents from headquarters, who were studying serial rapists in hopes of finding clues as to why serial rapists do what they do in hopes of coming up with ways they could identify men that may be prone to such traits. One such member of that team was William Carle of the Wilmington, Delaware Branch Office.

Fred stated that he was sorry that he had done the rapes and the killings. "I attempted to stop many times; but I just could not stop myself. I know that you are thinking that it was simply a sex thing, but it was not. I got little pleasure out of the rapes. I can't explain why, but it wasn't a sex thing. I never raped any little boys or girls. I always knew that sooner or later I would be arrested. My only explanation is that it gave me control. I was in control."

A newspaper article was written in the Seaford Leader that the killer of Harriet O'Brien, Jeanne Records, Rosalie Ellis, and Jennifer Collins was sentenced to life imprisonment and that Horace Hastings was totally innocent of all involvement in the deaths of Harriet and Jeanne.

Helen Carle made a contribution of $50,000 to the University of Delaware for tuition assistance to graduates from the Seaford and Laurel School Districts, and a contribution of a like amount to the Seaford Police Department for needed equipment.

Helen gave birth to a boy who she named William Robert Carle. Kathy Miller gave birth to a little girl that she named Helen Kathryn Miller.